THE RURAL
GENTLEMAN

"All great literature is one of two stories, a man goes on a journey or a stranger comes to town."

Leo Tolstoy

BY

DELIA MAGUIRE

Grosvenor House
Publishing Limited

The right of Delia Maguire to be identified as the author of this
work has been asserted in accordance with Section 78
of the Copyright, Designs and Patents Act 1988

The book cover picture is copyright to Delia Maguire

This book is published by
Grosvenor House Publishing Ltd
28-30 High Street, Guildford, Surrey, GU1 3EL.
www.grosvenorhousepublishing.co.uk

A CIP record for this book
is available from the British Library

ISBN 978-1-78148-972-7

Prologue

There is a particular kind of history that lurks in the back of beyond; some of it sordid, much of it depressingly insular and parochial – but that is no excuse for historians to ignore it. This was the thought that preoccupied Barnabas Salmon as he drove from Cork city towards West Cork, with its isolated peninsulas and scattered island communities. Further- more, he ruminated, when it does make the written page, it usually gets confined to the realms of historical fiction where it is dismissed as a squalid and sleazy tale from long ago and far away. He glanced sideways at the surrounding undulating fields, still shrouded in the early morning mist and, unbidden, the dramatic words of Sherlock Holmes drifted into his mind, "the lowest and vilest alleys in London do not present a more dreaded record of sin than does the smiling and beautiful countryside." Well, writers would know, Salmon thought cynically, but the trouble is, while the stories some tell are historical, they are not necessarily fictional. More than that, the very precepts they uncover, frequently turn out to be the cornerstone upon which modern society is based.

There is without doubt something ethereal about the route Barnabas Salmon was travelling along, and many people who have travelled that same road can attest to its ghostly atmosphere and invitation to contemplation. Here, amongst the trees and roadside shrines, it is possible for even the most stoic traveller to be tranquillised into believing that they are progressing in the manner of Alice, when she pursued the white rabbit in a downward trajectory. Perhaps this is due to the kaleidoscopic effect induced by the ever-changing scenery, which frequently lulls the unsuspecting traveller into a sense of imminent discovery. It is a journey which combines past and present, as the modern road west unrelentingly cuts through occasional remnants of ancient woodlands, over the backs of old-fashioned bridges which, in turn, cross rivers that have flowed since history began. What is and what shall be.

Those who pass along this lonesome highway may think they are observing the picturesque scenery in relative privacy, but they are in fact observed themselves by the multitudinous crows and ravens who populate the entire region. They keep a sharp, inquisitive eye on the happenings of the road from their vantage point aloft the ever-increasing telegraph poles and wires. Only humans and primates can match these intuitive birds in their capacity to carry out sociable lies and deceptions. They watch and they remember.

The fairy tale depiction of a wild and isolated land, as once was true, is now no more than a wistful illusion when it comes to the small remote country towns and villages. These "once upon a time" sleepy hollows, formerly the preserve of family traders, have been transformed by the economic boom the country experienced in the early part of the 21st century. Nowhere is this new modernity more apparent than in the array of culinary delights available from even the most traditional of holdings. Frappuccino, kalamata olives and marinated bison have all made their way to provincial Ireland, and are as much a part of the modern makeover as broadband, smoking bans and rural isolation. The Tiger economy had left its imprint in a collective, silent, steel-willed determination that the stagnancy and complacency of former years will never be favourably compared to the advances that have been made. There will be no return to bacon and cabbage, apple tart and tea, or dinner in the middle of the day, no matter how poignant or indeed romantic the memory of them remains.

As the road gathers momentum, it eventually arrives at where the wild Atlantic fringes the much prized patchwork fields of West Cork. Farmhouses and gaily-painted cottages huddle against the hills overlooking the coastline, and pretty fishing villages nestle around tiny harbours. There is a similarity more in style than substance, between these domiciled villages and their counterparts across the sea in Devon and Cornwall. However, they are no longer the exclusive habitats of fishermen and farmers. Attracted by the quality of both light and air, a whole host of international writers and artists have been drawn to the area and, impervious to the fact that they will always be regarded as strangers, have made it their home in exile.

This is rural Ireland in its most concentrated form, far removed from the frantic pumping heart of the city. When summer slowly and subtly arrives, the surrounding hills and meadows become home to herds of indolent cattle, while cumbersome farm machinery takes a similar occupation of the narrow country roads. Both, unconsciously, are an evocative visual representation of the daily grind of life.

Since the apparition of the Tiger, there has been an upsurge in the number of equestrian animals taking residence in the vicinity, ranging from fine Arab thoroughbreds to mutinous looking donkeys and sturdy Connemara ponies. The former stare out impassively at a passing world far removed from the one in which they were bred to excel, and their gaze captures something of the nostalgia for a time that has gone, but can never be entirely forgotten.

Yet this land, picturesquely wild and cultivated by turns is defined by water, from the incorrigible Atlantic that washes up fiercely and persistently along the jagged coastline, to the endless rivers and streams that criss-cross the green and fertile fields. The pace of the latter is similar to the people who inhabit the land, being slow and measured in turns, yet overflowing with the potential to violently erupt, given enough provocation. The rivers, hailed by the ancient Celts as portals to the otherworld are frequently named after the goddesses of old, a reminder that the past, though gone, can never be completely erased. They alone recall the covert memories of times long since passed.

But in this new idiosyncratic age, the functional and sensible homesteads of the 21st century are built along the boundaries of gregarious babbling brooks - a vain attempt by cynical developers to grace them with a tinge of romance and mystery that the modern era derides and yet, simultaneously, secretly yearns to recapture.

It was in the midst of this quintessential rural Irish landscape, the county of General Michael Collins, and the town-land that suffered most grievously in the Great Famine, that Father Barnabas Salmon came to reside. He had retired from his role as a parish priest in a busy metropolitan area on the grounds of recurrent ill health and was to serve as the priest-in-residence in the rural parish of Droumbally. Though not a physically remarkable man, he was slightly taller than average and he did possess a naturally distinguished air. His bearing was straight, almost military in its demeanour, and it was set off by a neat cap of whitish grey hair, which fit his skull to perfection.

There were two things in particular which marked him as different from the men, and most especially the priests, of the locality, and one of these was the minor detail of his attire. He took great care with his appearance and was never seen without a brightly coloured silk cravat tied elegantly about his neck. In the winter months, he sported a dark overcoat, quite appropriate to his status as a clergyman, but for the rest of the year he donned a brown tweed jacket complete with leather elbow patches and a matching tweed cap. His attire, and his constant companion - a small Jack Russell cross terrier who the reverend (to the consternation of his pragmatic parishioners) named Wolf - all combined to give the impression of a man on a hunting mission. Plagued by an erratic heart and occasional bouts of breathlessness, Father Salmon was quite convincingly not an athletic man. Nevertheless, not a day went by when he was not seen traipsing the scattered rural sea-scape parish, dog by his side, doffing his cap in greeting whenever he met friend or stranger. He carried himself with the natural poise and ease of a Shakespearean actor treading the boards of a familiar stage, and this alone made him the target of much conversation and not a little good-humoured derision. The matter of his dress was trivial in comparison to the second astounding fact that marked him as unique. For as quintessentially Irish as the landscape was, so Father Barnabas Salmon was without equivocation, quite the most quintessential English gentleman.

No one knew for certain just how it came about, that a parish in the very heart of the rebel county, came to be the home of a retired tally ho English priest, and just who it was that was being punished; priest, parish or perhaps both.

Chapter One

The Salmon of Knowledge

Father Barnabas Salmon arrived at the parish of the Faithful Virgin on the first day of May 2007, and the mystery of his sudden arrival was matched only by the abruptness of his departure on the feast day of the Good Thief, some three years or so later.

He had arrived in style into the village of Droumbally on a bright spring morning. Scant attention, or so he believed, had been paid when he had driven into the village in a classic British open top sports car. To be sure, most had taken him to be just an early tourist, but his presence, like that of any outsider, had been noted all the same.

The route south westwards had profoundly touched him. So much so, in fact, that along the way he had frequently paused at many of the roadside shrines and memorials to the men who had fallen in skirmishes leading up to that long ago declaration of independence. Before setting out, he had made it his duty to familiarise himself with the history of the area and indeed with the social history of Ireland in general. Consequently, he had spared more than a passing thought for all who had passed along that same road, driven from their homes, either as a result of famine or personal tragedy. A few days after his arrival in the small village, and from the comfort of the small chintzy bedroom that had been allocated to him, he had replayed the memory of the journey backwards in his mind. In his imagination, he had visualized the various town lands he had passed through, as possible one-time staging posts on a long and difficult journey. And in the quiet of his mind he questioned the possibility of the road he had travelled along, being similar in ambience to the one Leo Tolstoy had envisaged when he set his masterpiece Anna Karenina in an area that had once served as a remote dropping off point for prisoners on their way to Siberia. A road which had subsequently become known as the Road of Tears.

His journey that May morning in 2007 had ended when he had pulled up outside an austere looking presbytery, a large double fronted house that had been painted a pale lemon colour many years previously. He had collected a small, dapper bag from the boot of the energetic looking little car, and had made his way up the steps to the dour looking Georgian front door. Waiting on the doorstep and unaware that he was being observed, he had adjusted his cravat and his smile, hoping it would not betray his wariness, and had waited patiently for the door to his new life to be opened.

It had not taken long for rumours to seep through the cracks and crannies of the old parochial house that the incumbent parish priest, Father Donal Ryan had not taken favourably to his new assistant. The parish priest was a native of the area, invested in both its structure and economy. His family had owned one of the larger farms on the outskirts, and two of his four brothers still owned and worked a massive acreage between them. Apart from his priestly duties, the rather sour faced Father Ryan was a great devotee of greyhound racing, and rarely missed a Saturday night meet at the stadium in Cork city. He exuded an old world mentality, and yet for all his old-fashioned cautious ways, he was one of the most avid recipients and users of the newly introduced broadband technology. Relying on his own ingenuity, he had quickly mastered this new tool. To the chagrin of the pastoral committee who thought the point of it had been to set up a parish database, he had prioritised it almost exclusively for the retrieval of race results, and details of forthcoming meets in Cork and Limerick.

He was, according to the sages of the area, now saddled with a frightfully proper English 'chap' who patronised and chided him about his hobby, and was forever seeking to correct the relaxed ways of the faithful old pastor. Reality should never be allowed to get in the way of a good story, but this calls for an exemption. There was no animosity whatsoever between the two men, and while not soul mates, they managed to live together without rile or rancour. Father Salmon had the common decency not to flaunt how intrigued he was by the lifestyle of Ryan, which afforded him great interior amusement. He did wonder though, what the busy bodies who had often attempted to run his previous English parish would make of a priest who not only gambled but also was, by all accounts, a top rate tipster.

In turn, Ryan was secretly bemused by the spectacle of his new assistant with his clownish attire, teeth grinding accent and bizarre choice of reading material. He couldn't help but think there was something distinctly fishy behind the Bishop's decision to send him as he had put it 'the gift of Salmon,' but he was wise enough to know that all would eventually be revealed.

To the disappointment of the parish, the sports car was not a fixture. It belonged, apparently, to Salmon's sister, Clarissa, and a few days after his arrival, a handsome, debonair English gentleman arrived and drove the car back to England. After its departure, Salmon bought an old, rather sensible looking car which he seldom used, since his preferred method of transport was walking. On occasion, he tried taking out the High Nelly that belonged to Father Ryan, but proved a menace to himself since his balance was questionable. Forever in the memory of the village, he was recalled as the priest who had arrived topless on a warm spring morning...

Long before he celebrated his first Mass in Droumbally, word had travelled far and wide about the latest addition to the village. The idea of an English priest in such a small community was considered by many to be perverse, and even antagonising. Some remembered a popular television show from the latter days of the last millennium, that had featured an English priest, and which had started out as a comedy and ended up as a drama. The question on everyone's mind was; would life follow art?

However, the notion of an English priest made for a good topic of conversation and while some doubted the wisdom of such an appointment, most were content to be intrigued. There was only one parishioner who maintained a malevolent bitter attitude, and like many people who resist change in the church most strongly, Ger O'Reilly didn't even practice his religion. He farmed a smallholding on the outskirts of the village and supplemented his income by working occasionally as a labourer. His opinions, which he was always eager to share, were rarely sought, for his reputation as a harbinger of gloom generally preceded him.

Overhearing an exchange of banter concerning the accent of the new priest one night in O'Neill's bar, O'Reilly had felt irresistibly driven to making a comment. 'Bloody English,' he had contributed. 'The economy is up and what do you know, they are back, only this time they will have to buy houses not commandeer them as they used to.'

He was answered by Sheila O'Neill, the dark haired proprietor who ran the small bar, along with her big shambling husband, with a brusque efficiency. 'I can't see a priest being drawn here by the economy,' she had remarked, 'unless you think it's your land he's after, but sure Ger aren't you always in the field when luck is on the road?' She turned and winked at a tourist who stood by the counter with an almost empty glass in his hand, and a mournful expression on his face.

'I wouldn't put it past him,' O'Reilly replied irritably, 'and besides, I wouldn't want a bloody Brit praying over me or mine.'

'I shouldn't think he'd burst a gut wanting to either,' Sheila had retorted, watching as the tourist downed his glass, glanced disdainfully at O'Reilly, and then made for the exit. Turning to O'Reilly, she had addressed him crisply. 'It's time, Ger that the likes of you realised that some things are water under a ducks arse, because if you don't, the second millennium will never get off the ground in these parts.' And with that, she had shot him a contemptuous look, before wandering outside in order to smoke a cigarette in relative peace. Watching O'Reilly through the window as he exchanged words with another rotten history veteran, it occurred to her, that he was like a poorly trained guard dog seeing off the benign and inviting the malignant.

While Ger O'Reilly was alone in his vendetta of bitterness, many, maybe even the majority of parishioners, were suspicious of the new priest and queried the wisdom of him being sent amongst them. There were rumours that he was from a parish near London, and they wondered how he would ever adapt to such a small community, for they were, they liked to believe, a simple people happiest amongst their own.

Interest along with nosiness ensured that more people than usual turned up for Father Salmon's first Mass in the parish. Speculation about the sudden appearance of this strange priest had been rife, and many parishioners had crawled out of the woodwork drawn by curiosity, and a desire to witness the bizarre.

The congregation awaited the presence of the priest, and the commencement of the Mass with a sense of anticipation, but the moment the distinct clear diction of Barnabas Salmon wound its way round the building, they recoiled almost as if in shock. Did the man have any idea how peculiar his voice sounded? Did it even occur

to him that such a voice had never before addressed
them from that neat and familiar little altar? As the
Mass progressed, the mood and attitude amongst the
parishioners shifted in a more antagonistic direction, as
some perceived the priest to be arrogant in the way he
conducted himself. He stood tall and erect with his
head held high as he stared down at them from the safety
of the altar. The voice, so clear and so commanding,
induced more than one parishioner to make a secret vow
to march out should the words of his sermon match the
tone of his voice.

Father Salmon seemed oblivious to the sense and sensi-
bility of his congregation. He forsook the raised pulpit,
so favoured by Father Ryan, and walked to the centre
aisle of the church where he spoke the only way he knew;
from his heart and with a sense of purpose.

He didn't begin by offering a simpering word of
thanks to the gathered community for their reception
of him, which although it had been conducted within the
bounds of hospitality, had been noticeably lacking in
warmth, and in that instant he earned himself a grudging
measure of respect. At least he wasn't a sycophant. He
then proceeded to take the crowd unawares by launching
into an autobiographical description not so much
about who he was, but more particularly about where he
came from.

'I'm sure you have heard on the grapevine and now
have confirmed by your ears that I have come among you
from afar. I apologise in advance should my voice irritate
or aggravate you to distraction, there is a reason for it.

Many moons ago, when I was a young man and full of hope and ambition, I decided to become an actor. Well it was the 1960's and many angry young men in London and elsewhere were setting out to create a revival of the theatre. To be successful, and by that I mean to become a serious actor, one had to have voice training, so along I went and in due course I was taught pronunciation, intonation and voice projection, so that the darkest recesses of the theatre might be reached.

'I am not unaware of its ability to make people flinch, and I can understand how overbearing it might sound to people like you who are used to soft tones and lilting voices.'

A collective guilt descended on the congregation, who now felt willing to forgive the voice since its owner saw it as a vice rather than a virtue, and they settled to listen to him as if a story was about to be told rather than a sermon preached. It was clear that a serious deviation was evidently about to take place. Father Ryan and every priest that had ever served the parish in living memory had kept to a strict formula when it came to preaching. Usually, this formula involved a brief recap of the day's Gospel (with an occasional parable thrown in if it was a special feast day) followed by a rapid run through of the notices for the week all wound up by an impatient beckoning of the hand for the congregation to get back on their feet.

'I know it is Saturday night,' Salmon continued, 'and many of you are eager to be attending another venue nearby, but I would so much like to tell you about where I hail from and how I have accrued, over my life, the small amount of knowledge I possess. That way as I get to know you, you can rely on knowing something about me.

'I grew up in the years following the Second Great War – a description which I consider to be a contradiction since there is nothing great about war. I was born in 1943 and while I hasten to tell you that I am not a perfectionist, I really rather believe that my parents were.

'1943 was not a remarkable year, but two happenings of note did take place during it, and over the years, both have given me great cause for contemplation on a number of levels. The first one, which I shall come back to and deal with at a later date, was the creation of a spectacular plot devised by the British secret service which was hatched to deceive the Germans over the invasion of Sicily, and which became known as "the man who never was." The second one, an altogether more tragic affair was the mass execution of six members of the White Rose pacifist movement in Nazi Germany. You see, everywhere in life, even in the darkest of days there is evidence of heroic deeds.

'My memories are of a place full of great and gentle beauty, a quintessential English village that survives to this day as beautiful and idyllic as ever. It nestles between the city of Canterbury and the coastal town and port of Dover in the south east of England. I do not doubt for one moment that you all rejoice in belonging to the rebel county, and it is fitting that you should. I too take great delight in Kent, which is rightly known as the garden of England, even if, during the war, it was known as Hellfire Corner.

'As I paint before your eyes a picture of my childhood you may well think that it is nothing more than the ramblings of an old man, but childhood memories leave behind so much more than inconsequential thoughts. In fact, the older one gets, the haunts of childhood often beckon more urgently. I can recall in the blink of an eye the village green, the timber fronted houses, and the ancient old church that once was the heart and soul of the village.

'I have to acknowledge here and now that I have lived a privileged and charmed life. My sister Clarissa still lives in the beautiful environs of rural Kent and whenever we get together as all siblings in Christ should, we recall with joy and wonder the beauty that was our world.

'The writer Joseph Roth articulated something that is very close to my heart, when he said that before the First World War, it took a long time for someone's place to be taken after they had died. After the calamity of mass death and slaughter, life became expendable, more ephemeral, and I suppose cheap.

'The landscape of my childhood, as I recall it in the interior of my mind, is similar to the one Roth speaks of, that once existed long ago. Kent as you may well know is famous for its apple and cherry orchards, which I assure you, are a feast for the eyes in springtime, but it was also once famed as a hop growing area.

'Those of you who grew up in this area of outstanding beauty will retain forever in your heart and in the attic of your mind, the majesty of the mighty Atlantic, the rolling hills and picturesque meadows. As a man in the evening of life, I find comfort in recalling the charm and allure of my childhood, and I am saddened that the cult of indifference, which was unleashed by the atrocities of the twentieth century, far from diminishing with time, has in fact been elevated far beyond its merit.

'We all have a different life story to tell and much of it is dictated by circumstances of birth. I was blessed with a childhood that gave me access to so much sweetness and light, but I am aware that this is not the experience for everyone. When I was growing up, it seemed that those endowed with plenty got more, and that the rich and socially attuned were educated solely with a mind to taking their perceived rightful place at the helm. As for the poor, they were left to expect nothing but crumbs from the rich man's table. Has it changed, substantially I mean? But then as an Italian proverb has it, a king and a pawn go into the same box at the end of the game.

'But on this fine May evening, rather than dwell on thoughts of inequality which have the capacity to make me feel guilty, I would prefer to indulge in memories of long hot summer days, swimming in the river followed by picnics under the shade of the mighty oak, horse riding and cricket, and of course tea on the village green.

'As I mentioned, this was a hop growing area, and the harvesting of the crops was never a dull affair. I recall the Londoners from the east end and the gypsies who congregated in camps on the outskirts of the village; transient people who came every year to pick the hops, cheerful, loud and full of life. We children played together from sunrise to sunset, and amid all the fun and laughter, there was no such thing as rich and poor - only good and bad.

'The great French novelist Colette stated that a happy childhood is poor preparation for human contact. My dear people, who am I to judge such an accomplished writer? Even so I have to disagree with Colette, if only as a matter of self- preservation, but this is the critical thing I want you to remember from tonight onwards.'

At this point Barnabas Salmon paused, and for a moment looked into the congregation almost as if he were searching for someone, and not having found them, returned thoughtfully to his flow. 'Life is a beautiful gift from God and if there is anyone here tonight who was unfortunate enough not to have happy memories, remember this, it is never too late to have a happy childhood. I really rather hope this sentiment encapsulates what will be my mission amongst you.'

Chapter Two

Quality or Quantity

Childhood was a theme that Father Barnabas Salmon was to return to on several occasions. However, while the landscape he now inhabited had a mythical aura, it was in fact home to a stoic and pragmatic people who rarely indulged in otherworldly thoughts or fancies. Yet there was an allure about the man, owing perhaps to the contradiction that while he looked impassive, he sounded both emotional and caring. Many found themselves in the rather invidious position of desiring to hear more about something that made them feel both simultaneously intrigued and uncomfortable. There was something seductive about his interest concerning days gone by. It appealed to something deep in the subconscious of many Droumbally parishioners, and even though, upon reflection some felt duty bound to dismiss the enchantment he weaved, they were invariably drawn back to hear more about what Barnabas Salmon had to say.

It was deeply fortunate for the priest that the Ryan and Murphy reports into the abuse of children by members of the clergy had not, at this stage been published. If they had been, some parishioners would have taken issue, not only with Salmon's stance regarding childhood, but also with his right to express it. In the minds of some, those reports established beyond doubt that where children are concerned, priests are the very devil. Salmon elevated childhood to impossible heights, most especially his own, and exhorted fiercely the rights of the child. Above all, he abhorred the breaking of a promise to children.

'Do not break your word once you have given it to a child,' he once declared randomly at the end of a sermon. 'You may think it trivial, but a child never does; if you can't keep a promise, don't make one.'

It was when he made remarks like this, tersely and gruffly, in a manner at variance with how he had just spoken, that some people broke free, temporarily, of the hold he had over them and observed that there was possibly another side to this priest, one he was not so keen to publicise.

He cut a strange figure with his clear precise diction, and somewhat flamboyant style of dress, overwhelmingly cheerful in disposition, yet given to a sudden sharpness and sardonic turn of phrase when the mood took him. He was an enigma, speaking on the one hand with a surety of knowledge that was exceedingly comforting, and yet for a man of undoubted intelligence he revealed an astonishing failure to grasp local etiquette. Did it occur to him for example, that for people who rarely disclosed intimate details, most especially to strangers, that it was bordering on the embarrassing to hear a grown man talk about the year of his birth and teenage ambitions? He also displayed a mortifying level of naivety by speaking glibly about such things as boarding school and servants, in a manner that suggested he thought such experiences were commonplace.

He presented his parishioners with a dilemma for he encompassed all the ingredients that ought to make him thoroughly dislikeable, yet attraction prevailed. Step by step, the small insular community were inextricably drawn to hear the tales and descriptions of a world that was both alien and captivating. It was as if the pied piper had come amongst them.

Word began to spread fast, and in time, people who had ceased the practise of their faith or who had drifted to the town Mass which took place at more convenient times, felt inclined to witness what all the commotion concerning the new priest was about.

The teacher, Eddie Moran, was one such character. He was a dark haired sombre looking fellow who taught physical education at the community school in the town. Some three months before the arrival of Father Salmon, he had married his long-term girlfriend Carolyn O'Shea. They had met at school and Carolyn's father who was a well-known auctioneer and ambitious for his daughter, had fervently hoped that the relationship would peter out when Eddie had chosen to go to Limerick to study teaching, while Carolyn had pursued accountancy in Dublin. She had returned to take up a prestigious job at a bank in the town. A few months later, Eddie had secured a position at the town school, and the romance had continued from where it had left off. As the two of them approached their thirtieth year, the romance morphed into an engagement, and eventually marriage.

Their wedding, which Father Ryan had described to Barnabas Salmon in highly ambivalent tones, had apparently been one of the most spectacular events to have taken place in the parish for some time. No effort and most certainly no money had been spared in making it the local wedding of the decade. Several glamorous bridesmaids had been attired in designer gowns, and the guest list had included many unknown to either the bride or groom. A paternal uncle of Carolyn's, who was a priest in California, was flown in to concelebrate the nuptial Mass along with Father Ryan. He had been accompanied by several cousins who had never been to Ireland before, and they had returned home enamoured with the style of the old country. A honeymoon in the Caribbean followed the wedding, and the couple were presented with the keys of a fabulous house, a gift from Carolyn's disappointed parents. Right up to the last minute, they had made every effort to persuade their only daughter to rethink her decision.

Eddie Moran, captain of the school football team, and legendary class prankster in chief, had pursued and won the heart of the much sought after Carolyn, even though the massive odds of both class and background had been stacked against him. And yet when he had taken his place beside his new bride at the top table in the top hotel, far from being overwhelmed with joy he had been swamped with a sensation of boredom and indifference. The intensity of his feeling had frightened Eddie, for he was unfamiliar with strong emotions. Initially he had tried to dismiss his misgivings as nothing more than anxiety, and he had persuaded himself that all would be well once they reached the warmth of the Caribbean sun. However, far from diminishing, the anxiety had grown more intense. He arrived back from his honeymoon cutting an altogether more serious figure, which in turn afforded a measure of relief to his parents-in-law who mistook his new demeanour as a welcome sign of maturity.

Now, as he sat like a dutiful husband and son in law with his wife and her family at the Saturday evening Mass, his thoughts turned to his friends, who had travelled that very day in anticipation of the Cork hurling team winning in Dublin. He felt a huge surge of resentment. He flicked his eyes towards his wife, and noted how passive she looked. She only practised her religion because, like him, she was indebted to her parents, and he felt a frisson of dislike for her weakness.

His thoughts were interrupted by Father Salmon's loud voice. His irritation switched effortlessly from his wife to the priest, whose voice resounded in Eddie's ears like the commotion caused by numerous hungry birds demanding to be fed. It hammered through Eddie's consciousness and refused to be ignored.

The gospel reading had been about the wedding feast at Cana, and this alone had served to distance Eddie even further, for it reminded him of his own wedding feast, and the revelation that had left him standing on his head ever since. He closed his eyes and tried to focus on his secret thoughts. It was simple really, he told himself, he was no longer attracted to Carolyn, and he wondered if he ever truly had been. Other women didn't attract him either, so what was the issue? He wasn't a particularly analytical man, but he had an innate wariness of confronting something that might prove too complicated to handle. He glanced across at his wife again. Was it possible that she felt the same way, and was that why she kept herself surrounded by her family? Were they her metaphorical barge pole that she used solely for the purpose of keeping him at bay? The possibility did not offer him any relief.

He turned his head away and watched as the priest made his way to the central aisle in readiness to deliver his sermon. Everything about the man irritated Eddie Moran. Look at him, he thought, how pompous he is, how presumptive to imagine that people actually want to listen to what he has to say. He watched critically as the priest gazed out upon the congregation, turning his head from east to west like an actor preparing to enthral his audience.

'If you are afraid of loneliness, don't get married.'

For one terrifying moment, Eddie thought the priest was speaking directly to him, and he felt the pulse of his blood as it thundered through his ears.

'That was the opinion of Anton Chekov,' the priest continued, 'so do not dismiss the sentiment too easily. However, putting Anton aside for a moment let us get back to Cana. Take a moment, and think about how many times you have heard that reading over the years. Has it ever occurred to you to wonder what the happy couple who had just got married were actually like? Their families were obviously socially connected to the family of our dear Lord, and the connection was strong enough for his holy mother to be concerned about their social standing - hence her urgency in getting the wine to flow again. There is no doubt that then, as today, weddings are important occasions. We know all about the issue with the wine, and the slight contention between Christ and his Mother, but what about the couple themselves. They were the important players and yet of them, there is no mention.

'When I was young, I had the great good fortune to fall head over heels in love with a most wonderful young lady. It was no passing fancy, we were even engaged, and in some ways, it was like a 1960's Romeo and Juliet for neither family were bowled over by our decision. I am afraid the great British issue of class poked its rather annoying nose into our private business, and you do not need me to tell you, that snobbery is never ever remotely attractive.

'The issue you see, with both the story of Cana and my own experience, is that marriage, while involving two people is never just about two people. A lot of vested interests are involved when a wedding takes place, and the happiness or indeed misery that follows the exchange of wedding vows, never impacts just two people.'

The priest paused for a moment, and as he did so a few people took the opportunity to shuffle uneasily in their seats. It was a strange admission for a priest to make from the altar that not all weddings are inevitably followed by happy marriages. Eddie Moran, now far from disinterested, listened with rapt attention.

'Throughout my priestly ministry, I have always been aware that I look upon the whole subject of matrimony with slightly less rose coloured glasses than other priests. Perhaps this is due to my own very close brush with the state.

'Only a foolish person, or a very brave one, ever risks involving themselves in someone else's marriage; most of us settle for private conjecture.

'Some years ago I arrived at a new parish in the south of England, and I was asked by the adult children of a couple to bless their parents on the occasion of their fortieth wedding anniversary. Naturally, I was happy to oblige, and it was arranged for the blessing to take place the following Sunday. I hasten to add, in my defence, that I was new to the parish, and on my best behaviour, but even so that did not prevent me from putting my foot firmly in my mouth. I blessed and commended them and remarked to the congregation that in an era where some marriages do not last forty minutes, it was a tonic to witness one that had lasted forty years. Well that received a round of applause, and after Mass, we all gathered in the parish hall for coffee and biscuits.

'Now at the risk of sounding very churlish, or indeed judgemental, I have to confess something. This couple, who I did not know, were rather lacking in charm. The gentleman was stuffed with self –importance, and something of a buffoon, and his lady wife was domineering and abrasive. Several people, spurred on by Christian charity, offered their congratulations, only to be shown a cold shoulder. Apparently, you see, only the salutations of the high and mighty were acceptable. It was all quite unedifying and rather embarrassing.

'A young girl, late teens early twenties, who had been observing the whole performance, turned to me and, after giving me an uncomfortably quizzical look she said: '"Well Father with all due respect, forty minutes or forty years is all very well, but after watching this charade, I personally would settle for quality over quantity any day."'

A faint ripple of amusement ran through the church and he put his hand up to acknowledge it.

'I didn't have a ready reply. On reflection, of course, I could have told the young lady that it should never be a matter of "either or." There are short unhappy marriages, and long fulfilled ones, and vice versa. Nevertheless, she was quite right about the imperative of quality, and that aspect really is in the hands of the two people making the vow. It can only come about if the couple consciously place each other at the centre of their respective universes.

'I cannot finish without going back to Chekov. I have to say, loneliness is something that has always filled me with fear, but that isn't why I didn't go ahead and marry my great love. I would never have been lonely with her by my side. No, my dear friends, I never fell out of love. I simply had the great good fortune to hear a calling from the Lord, and when a man hears that call, then the nets must be left on the shore, the field left unploughed and the bride to be left unwed. Following the Lord is never easy, as another great writer put it, "the soul is always on it's knees."'

Chapter Three

Word Seeps Out

For some time after his sermon on matrimony, a cloud of scandal descended on Father Salmon. His revelation of having been in love scandalized some, amused others and gave rise to more than a few "nudge-nudge, wink-wink" comments amongst the rump. Moreover, his comments regarding quality versus quantity was deciphered by some as an endorsement of divorce and separation.

Madge Healy, a retired schoolteacher who lived opposite the presbytery, and assisted with much of the parish administration, quickly became Father Salmon's staunchest critic, following this sermon. Unlike the boor O'Reilly, her dislike was not motivated by a racist inclination, but quite possibly from an uneasy conscience.

It was common knowledge that her marriage had been a long and unhappy one. When her husband, who had been ten years her senior, had died in a freak sailing accident, she had been consumed with a confusing mixture of both grief and guilt, the latter being due to the overwhelming sense of relief she had felt. His untimely demise had released her from a life of tyranny at the hands of a jealous and unfulfilled man. What had contributed to the complicated mixed emotions was the realization that, for the first time in her adult life, she now had both money and the freedom to spend it. Her two sons had emigrated to New York on the cusp of the Celtic boom, and their decision to do so had mortified her. Both had graduated with good degrees in architecture, and had stood to gain significantly from the blossoming economy, but the prospect of staying local held no appeal for either. Nothing would entice them to stay in an area that held so many unhappy memories of their childhood, and they had left Madge without the fig leaf of a failing economy to excuse their choice.

Father Salmon's sermon, which acknowledged the very real reality of unhappy marriage, found no grateful recipient in Madge Healy. She had confided in various priests during different stages of her married life, and beyond sympathising, the best any of them could suggest, was that she offered her sufferings up as a penance. She took issue with Father Salmon's easy depiction of what constitutes a happy marriage, and as someone ashamed of her lonely existence, she silently bore him malice for his apparent approval of Chekov's pronouncement.

It was Madge who told Mary Regan about the disciplinary speech Father Ryan had launched on Father Salmon with regard to this scandalous sermon. Mary Regan was widely acknowledged by the older people of the parish to have a tongue that would clip a hedge.

The younger people generally referred to her as "the google" since she was a consistent source of news and gossip. She ran a small stylish boutique with the panache of an enterprise based in Bond Street or Rome, and frequently jetted about Europe in search of the latest fashion trends. Her exquisite boutique drew custom from far and wide for she had a natural flair and a commendable dedication to detail. Her business success had been aided and abetted by the twin benefits of having inherited property, and having had the good sense to marry a builder. This latter benefit was something her older sisters had both once found rather shocking and pitiful, since they had made it a priority to settle for professional men. Unknown to them however, Mary's husband Dermot was every bit as driven and talented as his wife. When the Tiger came a calling, Dermot had seized the opportunity and had transformed himself from a mere jobbing builder into a big time developer.

The Regans were no longer the poor relations. Mary Regan was now a very wealthy woman, but money had never assuaged her massive need to know what was going on in the locality. What better way was there to find out, than running an upmarket clothes shop frequented by people who were all going somewhere, be it weddings, funerals or interviews? They presented a captive audience as they perused the clothes rails, listening to Mary's flattery and discernment. She worked quickly, deftly filleting facts and occasionally figures, using the mechanism of laughter and light-heartedness to disguise the purpose of her chitchat. No matter how trivial, she swept all the information into her vast memory bank, with the ease of a fisherman tossing a gutted fish into a freezer.

Madge Healy was not a natural gossiper, but she was lonely and the moment she placed herself in Mary's capable hands it was inevitable that stories concerning the new priest would enter the public domain. An invite to the wedding of her niece in Carlow had put Madge in need of a hat. Within minutes, Mary had established that the niece in question worked for a bank, had endured a somewhat spiky romance, and was eager to move back to Cork.

'Let's hope she's had the good sense to settle for quality and quantity then,' Mary had laughed, and responding to what she considered was a throw away comment, Madge had replied. 'My God, what a way to sum it all up.'

'Isn't it though,' Mary had replied. 'Dermot said I'd a bargain in him seeing I got both quantity and quality, and I haven't the heart to tell him that I never could figure the difference between glitter and gold.' She paused and leaning forward, she adjusted the tiny-feathered hat that sat like a dead bird upon Madge's greying curls, and sliding effortlessly from fun to gossip she added: 'I wonder how poor Father Ryan puts up with it.'

'Well he doesn't,' Madge replied, anxious to protect her favoured priest from possible accusations of cowardice. 'He told him what is what in no uncertain terms.'

'Go away with you,' Mary had said incredulously, taking the hat away and exchanging it for a bold and fussy fascinator. 'What on earth did Father Salmon say to that, I can't imagine him taking it easy?'

Caught up in Mary's sense of drama, and not wanting to disappoint her, Madge gave a potted version of the conversation she had overheard. Only she didn't give an accurate one. Because, like most people who are concerned only with the letter rather than the spirit of the law, Madge heard with her ears, but did not decipher with her heart.

Father Ryan had addressed Barnabas Salmon about the sermon, even though the English priest had not said anything with which Ryan himself did not agree. In fact, nearly fifty years into his ministry, the thing that puzzled Ryan most, was the rising call for a married priesthood. The lunatics were most definitely running the asylum. Ryan had heard and witnessed so much distress from both husbands and wives over the years, that he had long ditched the idea that he had sacrificed a family in order to serve God. He couldn't help thinking he had dodged a bullet, and in that regard, his views on matrimony were a great deal more sceptical than those of the slightly younger priest, and oceans apart from the traditional stance taken by the likes of Madge Healy. His warning or advice to Salmon was not so much about the content, but the wisdom of telling parishioners too much about himself.

'You'll open yourself up to ridicule and scandal,' he told Salmon. 'In the main, these are country people, a lot of them are taking on the veneer of worldly wheelers and dealers because they have assets, but their hearts are not in it.'

'I have no appetite for scandal, I assure you,' Salmon had replied, 'but the truth is, you and I are not wet behind the ears types fresh from the seminary, and neither of us are under any illusions. A magnifying glass is being placed on the church in this country, with the lens becoming stronger all the time. If people do not like what they see, they will walk away; the record has to change.'

At this, Ryan had bristled slightly. He was not a combative man and he had an aversion to confrontation. He did his duty on Sunday, kept a tight fist on finance, and his nose out of private affairs. No one could accuse him of not practising what he preached, for he perceived his role as that of a messenger, and he never offered his personal opinion. However, it had irked him to hear the English priest talk about "this country". He had no more like or dislike of England than the average, but in the way many Irish people could stand the English football team, were it not for the English television commentators, he felt an instinctive irritation at what he assumed was natural British arrogance.

'Is the church thriving in England then, are the vocations swelling? Of course not, I'd take a wager that most priests either talk to empty pews or crowds of foreigners.'

Father Salmon looked aghast at his colleague. 'My dear man, I meant no insult and I apologise profusely if for one minute you think I am acting in a superior manner. The church in England is in free fall, but the two cannot be compared. Catholicism all but died in England some four hundred years ago, but here, until recently, it was the lifeblood of society. In truth though, I fear for its survival here more than almost anywhere else.

Faith prospers under persecution and I don't see persecution here, only indifference.'

'And talking about your own experiences will make an impact?' Ryan replied testily.

'Who can say,' Salmon replied, 'but it would be for the good if the people saw the church as being about the individuals that make it up, rather than as a faceless law ridden institution that makes or breaks them.'

'Well, let me tell you something,' Ryan had said, wishing to draw to an end a conversation that had become far too philosophical for his liking. 'Wait and see what they make of it, but with the exception of a few, your life story will have little impact. And, as for your quoting of foreign authors, that will only make some think you are just thick as thieves with the crowds from Eastern Europe who are flocking into the country like mice on the scent of cheese. I doubt most will make head or tail of what you are talking about, and perhaps that is just as well.'

The words echoing through the thick doors of the presbytery had sounded more acrimonious than they were. Ryan had only addressed the man because of Madge's perpetually concerned face, and with the mission accomplished, he had let the matter drop. Salmon recognised that the parish priest had to maintain some semblance of authority, and respected him for it. Neither had changed the heart or mind of the other, but then neither had set out to do so.

Chapter Four

The Selfish Midget

As the weeks and months flew by, Father Barnabas Salmon slowly slotted into the rhythm of the rural coastal community who accepted him rather like a visitor, someone to be tolerated, endured and charmed, all on the assumption that it was only a temporary imposition. There was a degree of wariness on both sides, tempered by instinctive hospitality on theirs, and a genuine desire for peace on his. Gradually his influence began to make itself felt, and the level of suspicion with which many had regarded him began to diminish. Some parishioners who had once been domiciled in England, or who had visited friends or family there, recognised many of the changes he made as fashions and habits shipped in from across the water.

One change of tradition Father Salmon quickly introduced, was the practice of greeting people after Mass. This soon put into jeopardy a long-standing custom common in many rural parishes, of small groups of men congregating in the outer porch purely for the opportunity to socialize. The group who hovered at the back of Droumbally church had skedaddled pretty niftily on the first occasion when he had descended upon them out of the blue, having glided up the aisle faster than a cat with its tail on fire. They hadn't even fathomed that the Mass was over and some had been engaged in a racy retelling of a scandal that was doing the parish rounds. Father Salmon, who had caught an exchange of profanities, had known immediately that the conversation had been less than charitable on all sides.

'Feathers are very hard to catch once they disperse to the wind,' he had remarked before proceeding to exit the church door. The men had looked blankly at one another, and Mossie O'Neill had made a screwing movement to the side of his head as an assessment of the mental health of the priest, and the rest had relaxed and nodded in agreement.

Most people were slightly unnerved by the prospect of shaking the hand of someone they had just heard preaching. Their reserve was not driven by dislike, but unease at the pure lack of necessity. Father Ryan never shook the hand of a parishioner; he didn't have to, they all knew not just him but his father, his brothers and his forebears. Other priests who had served the parish, but who had hailed from other areas, hadn't felt the need to ingratiate themselves; they had just got on with the job of being a priest. Why Father Salmon should think that acting like a politician was part of his priestly duties was beyond them.

Naturally, Salmon saw the whole deal from a different angle. If he was going to serve the parish, he had to find a handle on the people, and since they would naturally be reluctant about seeing him, the onus was on him to make the first move.

As with many new habits, it did not take long for this one to become a custom and most of the parishioners soon got used to the sight of him standing, hand outstretched beside the church door. The majority shook his hand, some dodged and weaved while others appeared to become remarkably devout, and took to remaining inside the church, deep in prayer, until the coast was clear and the priest had thoroughly disappeared.

Those who did engage soon discovered that he was indeed a man of the people, more so than the priests who followed sport and hung about the village bars. He knew intuitively whose hand needed shaking and more importantly that some declined not from hostility, but from an innate fear of revealing too much need for human contact.

His method of visiting parishioners also broke the established rules of the parish, and to the chagrin of Madge Healy, he ignored the rota that she had gone to great lengths to develop. In general, only the sick and those caring for them, who made a request, got to be visited. Salmon called not just on the sick but also the bereaved, the elderly and people who he personally identified as being in need of contact. Therefore, he called on new mothers, bachelor farmers and the early retired. Salmon took no heed of rules concerning his pastoral ministry, but followed where his instinct led him. In no time, he became a familiar sight, walking the countryside with his colourful cravat and peaked cap.

It was at O'Hara's farm that Father Salmon found his faithful companion. The O'Haras had always been regarded as a respectable, hardworking couple, until John O'Hara had been charged with leaving the scene of an accident under the suspicion of drunk driving. They now had pariah status, and life for their two young sons, who attended the village National school, was widely reported to be difficult. On top of that, the relationship between John O'Hara and his wife Sandra had become fraught and acrimonious. Salmon had made the decision to visit them following his visit to John O'Hara's victim, a middle-aged man who was surprisingly more charitable towards the plight of O'Hara than the wider community was inclined to be.

The first time Father Salmon had darkened their door, the O'Haras had felt awkward, wary and half inclined to think that he was calling to preach them a lesson on citizenship. It soon became abundantly clear that far from setting out to lecture, he had come to offer the troubled family the hand of solidarity. They grew to welcome his visits and to rely on him for a clear and unbiased opinion. It was the O'Haras who gave Salmon a small liver and white Jack Russell pup of dubious parentage, which the priest promptly called Wolf, a name he said would help the pup combat his runt status.

He was an unfailingly cheerful visitor, and although many people initially grumbled when they saw the priest and dog approaching their abode, not one ever felt worse for having spoken to him.

But for all the welcomes that Salmon soon accumulated, there was in the vicinity one person who the parish as a whole felt the Saxon priest should avoid, and this was Bridie Clancy, or as the village generally referred to her, the selfish midget.

Clancy lived in what had been a fine old house on the outskirts of the village, and since she never accepted visitors, she lived in splendid isolation. She was a tiny and thoroughly unpleasant, dislikeable old woman who had brought trouble and strife to most of her neighbours. As the years had gone by, her face had been ravaged both by age and a permanent state of perpetual rage, and the local population avoided her at all cost. Her husband, whom she had married in her middle years, had died some years previously, and the general opinion was that it was immaterial as to whether Charlie Clancy had gone to heaven or hell, since either would be preferable to living with Bridie. Charlie's family, unable to bear the thought of Bridie re-joining him in death, had broken with tradition and had taken him to be buried in the family plot on the outskirts of the local town from where he had originated.

While Bridie Clancy had let her husband's family take his body with relative ease, she would have dismantled the house stone by stone rather than let them have access to that. An uncle of the late Charlie Clancy had bequeathed him the house, which in its day had been a fine looking farmhouse, but now lay neglected and dilapidated. The same, however, could not be said of the gardens for they were full of mature trees, blossoming shrubs and beautifully tended flowerbeds full of colourful and fragrant blooms. A white magnolia tree grew by the gateway and it welcomed the arrival of spring every year, without fail, with an abundant display of beauty that was the envy of every gardener in the vicinity. The flowers in Clancy's garden were objects of temptation for many children who longed to gather a bunch of them to present to either a mother or a favoured teacher. Nevertheless, not one of them dared to trespass on Bridie Clancy's land for fear of coming into contact with her, and she had been christened 'the selfish midget' long ago by a neighbour who was familiar with Oscar Wilde's tale about the Selfish Giant who had also possessed a magnificent garden and malevolent attitude. It wasn't just children who were afraid of Bridie, even some adults secretly believed she carried the power of the evil eye and so avoided any personal contact with her.

In due course Father Salmon was given a full account of old Bridie not only from Madge Healy, but also by Father Ryan.

'You'll have to tread carefully,' Ryan informed him, 'she comes to Mass occasionally, I heard that she walked out of your first one, but there is nothing unusual about that. She comes and goes as she pleases, but she has a fierce hatred of priests and she'll bring a tear to your eye by the time she's finished with you if you intrude upon her, so be warned.'

Madge Healy dutifully backed up the parish priest. 'I'd stay away Father,' she advised. 'Bridie isn't shy about asking for help if she needs it and she has a wicked tongue in her mouth.'

Salmon had indeed spotted the old woman walking out of the church during his first Mass. The story concerning the bitter and obstinate old woman cutting her nose off to spite her face touched his heart, and filled him with a deep and overwhelming sadness that had chilled the very rafters of his soul.

'Was she ever any different?' he asked Madge one day.

The woman shook her head. 'Not that I can remember,' she informed him. 'Poor Father Ryan tried to visit her one Christmas and all he got for his efforts was a scolding, but then what would you expect out of a pig but a grunt? I remember hearing that there were rumours of a scandal about her and you know what they say about mud sticking.'

'Ah yes,' he had replied drily, 'mud and shit' nothing sticks quite like those two culprits.' And with that he had walked away, leaving a thoroughly disgusted Madge glaring at his departing back, thinking how typical it was of a toff to think they could use words from the gutter with impunity. You would never hear the likes of Father Ryan speak like that, she had told herself, conveniently forgetting how Father Ryan had once turned the air blue when Ger O'Reilly's overgrown Alsatian had stood on his sandaled foot, sending his ingrowing toenail even further into the abyss.

The Saturday following this exchange with Madge, Barnabas Salmon had hardly been able to contain himself when it came to the sermon. The information given to him by both Ryan and Healy had opened his eyes to what he considered was a strong fault line running through the small community; the impact of gossip, and the threat of scandal that blighted the lives of so many.

He had witnessed it first-hand the day he had intruded upon the conversation being held at the back of the church amongst the gossiping farmers, where he had distinctly heard the O'Hara family being discussed. The problem had become increasingly apparent the more parishioners he visited throughout the parish.

'My dear friends,' he began, 'I have been with you now some six months and I hope the burden of carrying me is not proving too heavy. Spring came and went in the blink of an eye, and my first summer in West Cork flew more swiftly than a wild swan.

'Autumn is here and the days are getting shorter and winter will soon be upon us and it is fitting that the subject I want to address tonight is a dark one that affects us all in one way or another.

'Socrates is reputed to have said that strong minds discuss ideas, while average minds discuss events, and weak minds discuss people. Now I am no philosopher, but I suspect there is more than a grain of truth in the great man's words.

'Gossip and scandal are two forms of entertainment which present a gateway to grave unhappiness, and I would suggest even outright evil. Much of the hurt we remember and carry over from childhood is bound up in things people said, and the injustice that was never corrected. Certainly, from my own schooldays I can recall instances of great pain inflicted on the innocent by the unthinking.

'What always amazes me is how ambivalent sentient humans can be on this subject. You see, the reality is - gossipers frequently speak about someone they hardly know, as if they were experts on that person's life.

'There are, of course, sound theological grounds for identifying gossip as a source of evil. Speech is a gift of the good Lord, and it hardly behoves an English man to remind Irish people about the power of the spoken or indeed written word. It is a poisonous enterprise that seeks to build oneself up whilst knocking another down.

'The tongue is referred to by St James as a fire, and as we know, fire not only burns but it spreads rapidly. The potency of gossip is, I believe, even more poisonous in a small community, because privacy is more difficult to maintain when, by necessity, you have to be able to rely on your neighbour.

'Scripture tells us that a good name is to be chosen over riches, for money can be replaced but a good name ruined; well how can it be retrieved?

'As rural people I have no doubt that most of you hold the fox to be a scurrilous creature. He slinks onto your property and thieves without mercy. Yet the fox must eat. What excuse is there for anyone to steal the good name of another, when they cannot know the true full story of someone else's life?

'Gossiping is every bit as brutal as hitting a defenceless person, but most gossipers would be outraged if it were suggested that they are common thugs.'

There was a general air of unease amongst the congregation. The voice of the priest was calm and clear as usual, but the more discerning listeners were aware that there was the faintest trace of an edge to it. His message drove home, and though one or two people winced as it occurred to them that he might actually be talking directly to them, the majority considered that they knew exactly who he had in mind, and it most certainly wasn't them.

'Remember,' he continued, 'gossip is not like a snowflake, it does not just disappear, it lingers, even the type that passes as humour. You know the kind I mean, "My, he provides a grand laugh the way he stumbles after a few drinks." The same goes for any story containing the dreaded word "but" which invariably implies an opposition is following on from a compliment.

"He's a lovely man but has a terrible temper," or "she is a great teacher but how did she get that job?"

'As you know by now, I view childhood with much nostalgia, but there is one aspect of it which we should grow out of, and that is telling tales. "Curse the whisperer and deceiver for he has destroyed many who were at peace." These are my sentiments but not my words, they come, of course, from the good book itself and we should all heed them. Tale bearing is quite possibly the wickedest form of gossip. All it ever leaves in its wake is loneliness and bitterness.

We are instructed by the good Lord to be as wise as serpents and harmless as doves. Being human is a balancing act, and we have to keep our wits about us and recognise the world we live in, but play by the rules of the world to which we aspire to belong. Be vigilant, not just in what you say, but in what you do. As some philosopher or other once said, "If I maintain my silence about my secret, it is my prisoner, if I let it slip from my tongue, I am its prisoner."'

Generally it was a trait of Father Salmon to end his sermons with either a touch of humour or something slightly irreverent. It was the clearest indication that preaching was over, and was as much as anything, the stamp of his particular style of delivery. No one really understood why he did it, or whether it was indicative of something they hadn't yet fathomed about the priest.

Jerh Lyons, an assistant bank manager who was also responsible for the parish choir had a theory. 'The man is pure actor,' he asserted, to the small group who had turned up one night for practice. 'The man doesn't preach, he performs.'

This analysis did not go down well with Meg O'Reilly, a newly joined member of the choir, and niece of the pugnacious Ger O'Reilly, who was still reeling at the effrontery of an English priest daring to put his feet under the table of a West Cork parish.

'I think that is a bit demeaning Jerh,' she said, 'he only wanted to be an actor in the way some boys want to be train drivers, it was a fad. I think he puts a lot of thought and energy into his sermons, and I'm glad he is proving my uncle wrong.'

'Oh I agree,' Lyons confirmed enthusiastically, 'it's always good to prove old Ger wrong, but isn't Salmon just a tad bit too theatrical?'

'He'd have you for that "but" Jerh,' commented Declan Pryce with a laugh, and the whole assembled group joined in, even Meg who had been quite annoyed at Jerh's assumption that it was quite acceptable to bait old Ger - only the O'Reilly' clan had the right to do that.

Her uncle and his racism was becoming something of an embarrassment. It wasn't just directed towards the priest, but also to the ever expanding numbers of foreigners including as he put it, the plastic paddies who, in his opinion, were taking over Ireland. Meg had tried arguing with him, but he remained adamant. "No one is Irish or has a right to be in Ireland unless they, their parents and their great grandparents were born and raised here." He had finished his tirade with a cruel and cutting comment about the Saxon priest, but his jibe had backfired.

Meg, who had rarely attended Mass since going to secondary school, had felt driven to see what the commotion about Father Barnabas Salmon was all about, and in the process had been thoroughly won over. She was attending choir practice, because when Salmon had heard that she wanted to be a singer, he had shared with her his theatrical ambitions of long ago. He had also revealed an astonishing level of knowledge about the various pop singers who had started out from church choirs. In Salmon, she had an ally, and she would brook no criticism either from her uncle or from Jerh Lyons.

'But,' Jerh reiterated, with the clear intention of clearing his name.

'Ah stop digging and start singing Jerh,' Meg told him dismissively, 'you know full well what Father Salmon said about "but." The priest is a good fellow. When was the last time any of us remembered a sermon, never mind discussed one?'

No one contradicted Meg, and a general consensus at the choir rehearsal was agreed. Father Salmon provided food for thought and though he might be guilty of other things, boredom certainly wasn't one of them.

Not long before Christmas Father Salmon informed his parishioners that he was going to England. His beloved Clarissa was ill and he had to attend to her.

'Behave yourselves while I am away,' he instructed his congregation mischievously, 'and I will try to do the same.'

Chapter Five

Yesterday Always Makes a Comeback

It was only after Father Barnabas Salmon had taken his leave, that many parishioners realised that, not only had they grown to tolerate the English gentleman, they had also grown to like him.

Naturally, there were some who were relieved to be greeted again by Father Ryan and his whistle stop tour of the Mass, but there were also others who felt a profound sense of disappointment. It was true that the parish priest exuded reliability, for with him, one Mass was much the same as another, but for some this no longer provided comfort. They recognised now that Father Ryan had a formulaic approach, but in contrast to Salmon, it felt quite predictable and monotonous. As for the way he read the notices, that could only be described as a back to school moment, for he read them with the same unquestioning authority of a head teacher addressing a school assembly.

There was never any possibility that Ryan would reveal something personal about himself, or ever confess to any fears or doubts he might once have experienced. He didn't hold with what he called the cult of personality, but even amongst those who hadn't warmed to Father Salmon, there wasn't one who believed that the English priest had set out to develop himself as a personality. From the outset, Salmon had presented himself as he was, comfortable in his own skin, and not out to win the parish over. His view seemed to be that he was just another priest in a long line of others who had gone before him, and in good time, he too would be replaced.

But to this parish, he was not just another priest. He was engaging with them as people, giving them an insight into another world, another way of being, and some intuitively felt that he was holding a mirror up to them. There had, of course, been other memorable priests in the history of the parish. There was one who had been known to have a very intense relationship with alcohol. And another who had been a vicious brute of a man from the locality, with a vindictive tongue who had set about preaching the gospel by demonstrating on a daily basis how not to live it. Irish fiction is full of such characters, priests and holy people behaving badly, overly pious or plain disinterested. They feature because they were and in some cases, still are, a reality, and no one is truly shocked when they encounter such poor examples.

There was a unique quality about the character of Barnabas Salmon and, without exception; no one in the parish had ever encountered a priest quite like him. In an inexplicable way, he brought with him a vibrant sense of expectation.

Barnabas Salmon returned to the parish some ten days later looking refreshed, invigorated and most flatteringly, very pleased to be home. His first duty had been to call at the home of Sam Dunne, a retired farmer who lived with his daughter and son-in-law. He had first visited Sam a few days before he had received the call summoning him to England. It had been a brief, chance visit, but Salmon had left the farmhouse under the impression that the old man wanted to speak to him in confidence, but a suitable opportunity hadn't arisen. Sam's son-in-law, Noel, now worked the farm and his daughter Anne worked for the council in the accounts department. Anne and Noel had one child, a son who attended the local National school. Much as Sam loved his grandchild he knew that, in days gone by, Julian would have been labelled as a sissy, for he was a very particular little boy. From the day the child had been born, he had lived by the adult mantra of "a place for everything and everything in its place," and his playtime, along with all his books were rooted in practical reality. There was a story in the village, that the parents had given the child a bicycle for his eighth birthday on the strict instruction that he was only to ride it around the big barn, since neither of his parents could tolerate the idea of the shiny toy being splattered with mud or other debris.

Sam believed that Julian's refinement was part of his daughter's wish fulfilment for the future. Anne was a very fastidious woman who grumbled at the cows for doing what comes naturally. He suspected that she had a secret determination that her son would not follow his father and grandfather into farming, and that the best way to secure this outcome was to make the child as docile and orderly as possible. The house was kept in a permanent state of perfection, with not even so much as a spoon ever out of place, and in this endeavour, she was well matched by her husband, a man who liked order every bit as much as she did. They were a stout and slightly morose couple, and Father Salmon's first thought on meeting them had been "well that certainly debunks the theory about opposites attracting."

Barnabas Salmon was fascinated by the habits and rituals of what he thought were a pair of tin soldiers. He was bemused as to how the easy going Sam Dunne could ever have reared a daughter like Anne, who in turn could tolerate a husband like Noel. Sam Dunne was a whiskery stooped little old man with a raucous laugh, a chesty cough, and a habit of spraying saliva every time he opened his mouth. Anne repeatedly reprimanded him about his manners but he still wore his boots into the house and spat freely and accurately into the open fire. The first time Salmon had called to the house, he had been horrified to see Sam sat at the table with newspaper spread all about his chair.

'These carpets are fierce hard to clean,' Anne had said when she saw the look on the face of the priest, 'and I don't want Daddy to be worrying about them.'

The old man had thrown his head back and laughed uproariously, showing a full set of missing teeth. 'Doesn't she have a great sense of humour Father; imagine me worrying about an old bit of carpet?'

Salmon had sat himself down at the table, and Anne had somewhat begrudgingly poured him a cup of tea.

She was not keen on clergy at the best of times and it irked her that this fastidious looking priest had witnessed her being pernickety.

'Well,' the priest had said, helping himself to sugar, while rejecting the milk, 'you look in great health Sam, no doubt you are being looked after splendidly.'

'Oh boy but I am,' the old man laughed. 'Anne treats me like a king, which is a grave pity since I am a peasant at heart and like a pig, I am only happy when I'm knee deep in sh...'

'Daddy I think Father Salmon catches your drift.'

'Oh Salmon, what a name,' the old man cackled with delight. 'I'd say you're a grand catch for the parish.'

Father Salmon nodded and laughed heartily to show appreciation of the old man's joke before stopping, and looking deadly serious for a moment. 'I'm afraid I am perfectly useless at fishing,' he said, 'I even rang up the fishing helpline for advice and asked them for a few tips, and the fellow said, "yes, can you hold the line," and I said no.'

Sam Dunne caught the joke immediately, and at once a shower of tea and soda bread sprayed over the table. Anne, who didn't have the faintest idea about what was so funny about ringing a help line, looked on aghast as crumbs and debris continue to float in the air straight from the old man's mouth. She immediately began to clear the table sending a clear signal that break time was over.

When Father Salmon had eventually taken his leave, he had walked back to the presbytery feeling the weight of the world on his shoulders. The plight of the elderly had long troubled him. He believed that the media, and the world in general, often presented them as a homogenised group when the reality was that their needs were as wide ranging as the rest of humanity. There were those who had grown old alone, living out their days in isolation, some in the back of beyond, some next door to busy young families who were not even aware of their existence. In his past parish in the South of England, visiting the elderly in care homes had almost driven him to despair. He had met in them countless old people who had once held positions of authority, and who had been left behind like toys that had outgrown their use. The story of such people was well documented, but people like Sam Dunne fell through the cracks, for on the face of it he was cared for, fed and watered, warm and dry with his family all about him. Yet the old man enjoyed an existence akin to a Christmas tree that had outlived its relevance. He had been stripped of his dignity, because he did not fit in with the new generation. What was theirs now had been his first. What was to be done? Anne and her husband Noel were unlikely to change, for they were new fogeys of the worst type, who appeared to expect an elderly man to adapt to the finesse demanded by the Celtic Tiger, who everyone with a brain knew was only visiting.

Given that the old man had played so much on Salmon's mind, it was natural that after arriving back from England he had headed straight to Sam Dunne. As it turned out Anne, Noel and Julian were out Christmas shopping in Cork. The old man waved him in enthusiastically.

'Well Sam,' he said, seating himself down at the kitchen table, 'I see Anne and Noel have been busy, that is a fine crib you have. You know when I went away, there was not a sign of Christmas to be seen, and in the last day or so the entire village is heaving with decorations.'

The old man nodded his head and the priest noticed for the first time that Sam was not as jovial as he remembered him being. 'I trust you are keeping well Sam,' he asked, 'eating properly and getting plenty of rest.'

'My God,' the old man sighed. 'When do I ever get the chance not to eat properly, I'm like a bloody horse, fed nothing but oats and apples. Who'd think the day would come when a heart could grieve for the lack of bacon and cabbage?'

'Remember this Sam, only a fool argues with a skunk, a mule or a cook,' the priest declared with a laugh. 'And while we're on the subject of eating, I heard a tale back in Kent about an old fellow who went to the doctor with a cucumber stuck in each ear and some cherries stuffed up his nose. He told the doctor that he felt simply terrible, and the medic replied, "of course you do my poor fellow, I can see you are not eating properly."'

The farmer laughed, and for a moment or two, the familiar gleam of devilment returned to his eyes. It didn't stay there long.

'To tell you the truth Salmon, I never thought the day would come when I'd talk my business through with a priest, and an English one at that, no disrespect, you understand, but I am worried.'

'Really Sam?' the priest replied. 'Is all well with Anne's job? I know she was under pressure with talk about relocation, but the farm looks well and I saw Julian in school earlier today, he was in fine form.'

'The farm is well enough thank God,' the old man replied, 'and nobody will prise that job away from her, but both her and him are infected with this building obsession that is going on all over the place. What with one thing and another, they want to mortgage the farm and build on the land.'

'Oh I see. I take it you are not happy with the plan, is it so very risky?'

'What in the name of God do a clerk and a small time farmer know about development?' he asked, as if exasperated with Salmon's foolishness at not grasping the insanity of it all. 'They are comfortable; they have no need for this malarkey.'

'I take it they are seeking proper advice,' Salmon asked, 'they are not being hoodwinked by some hood of a broker who has just set up as an advisor? A lot of that is going on right now.'

'Oh, you may be certain sure that Anne will investigate, she holds an inquisition into a missing orange from the fruit bowl, and a post mortem if Julian so much as farts out of line.'

'Then why are you so worried?'

'Well, you tell me Father, you are an educated man - do you think the boom can go on forever?'

'I might be educated, but I'm not a business man,' Salmon replied, 'but my instinct is that yesterday always makes a comeback. The Polish have a saying, "in just two days' time tomorrow will be yesterday."'

'Never mind about the Poles and their sayings,' the old man grumbled, 'right now all they are good for is taking other people's jobs.'

'Well Sam, I am quite shocked with you,' Salmon said pretending to be stern. 'I never had you as someone to begrudge another for seeking a better life; the Irish do it all the time and quite rightly.'

'Only because your crew came over here and put eternal flight on us all.'

'Now don't be getting personal Sam,' the priest replied. 'A small country will always have emigration, but I concede quite definitely that the English did more than their fair share to damage the Irish economy.'

'And now to rub salt into our wounds they send the likes of you to teach us the error of our ways.'

'Unfortunately, that is so.'

'Well thank God for it,' the old man replied, 'and you haven't fooled me Salmon, I know what you are doing, distracting me from my worries, I can read you, you know.'

'I wouldn't doubt it in the slightest,' Salmon assured him, 'and what a story I must be.'

Salmon had taken his leave from Sam Dunne in reflective form. He hadn't been in the least bit insulted by the old man's teasing banter, but more than that, he respected his viewpoint. Barnabas Salmon had studied enough history to know that England had a legacy in Ireland that was far from benign, and nowhere near being worked through. He did question, though, whether the Irish fully understood the depth of their antipathy towards Britain. Very often he thought they were inclined to pass insults off as jokes without ever questioning just how sincerely they held to the notion expressed in the joke. He found the Irish friendly, outgoing, kind-hearted and warm, but he found himself questioning the depth of their sincerity not so much on account of the outsider, but mainly with regards to how they treated each other.

He recalled the time he had attended an ecumenical conference in Dublin in 1990. The Irish had just beaten Italy in a football match, and the outpouring of spontaneous joy and pride had overwhelmed him. He wondered if the miracle was to be repeated in 2007, would the same level of excitement be shown? The new prosperity had changed outlooks; in many cases for the better, but it had been his experience that where there is money to be made, it will always result in each man for himself.

But then Irish history was a series of long tough battles and looking at it in religious terms, he saw it as a nation carrying its own particular cross. They would fall and rise and fall again.

A few years before Salmon's arrival in Ireland, a report into the diocese of Ferns had been published, detailing abuse committed by the clergy, and while Salmon had been sickened by its contents, they had not shocked him. More reports were due, and in his opinion, they would all contain more of the same, evidence of the Irish capacity to betray and hurt each other.

This was at the heart of his assessment of how the Celtic Tiger would end. Many people would be hurt, broken and sold out, because they were being played as a game by others who were out for themselves.

Intuitively, he knew quite well that Sam Dunne was not worried by the financial implications for Anne and her family should she and Noel delve into property development. They were too shrewd as a couple. They would take advice, build and probably sell before the crash. However, being pragmatic people who had indoctrinated their child with the philosophy of a place for everything and everything in its place, they were hardly likely to put up with an old man who stood as a grim reminder of their ancestry. They feed him like a horse, Salmon thought wryly, and no doubt when the time is right, they will put him out to grass like one too.

Chapter Six

Christmas Past and Christmas Present

When Barnabas Salmon informed his parishioners at the Christmas midnight Mass that he loved Christmas with all the intensity of a young child, there wasn't a single member of the packed congregation who doubted the truth of that statement. His boundless enthusiasm and determination to seek the positive struck many as quite childlike in its vehemence. Edel Murray, a retired hotel housekeeper who had taken on the role of providing an evening meal and carrying out small housework duties for the two priests at the presbytery, testified to this eagerness.

Father Ryan was quite particular, trimming his meat of all fat and never shy about commenting if it had been over or under seasoned. On the other hand, Father Salmon never questioned what he ate; rather he bolted his food with the gusto of a starving child just stopping short of licking the platter clean. Sometimes, the sight of this made Edel feel unaccountably sad, and on one occasion, when Father Salmon had caught her eye after retrieving a piece of sausage that had fallen to the floor and popping it into his mouth, he had remarked with a twinkle in his eye: 'Take no notice of me, Edel. Where food is concerned, I'm with Mark Twain, "eat what you like and let the food fight it out inside."'

The Christmas midnight Mass was usually the preserve of the parish priest; however, Father Ryan had been gripped by a flu virus that had left him in a state of some weariness. He decided after some debate that it would be better to break with tradition, and celebrate the Christmas Day noon Mass instead.

Christmas Eve night proved to be a clear cold one with temperatures set to drop in the early hours of Christmas day. Father Ryan had a good reputation for not stinting with the heating and with the large crowds, the chill of the night was kept at bay. There was an undeniable spark of excitement, with many wondering just what kind of spin the "rural gentleman" would put on the great feast.

It was Patrick Moriarty, the postman, who bequeathed this nickname for Father Salmon, and once it was coined, the name stuck. Moriarty had said that the sight of the priest in his tweed jacket and cap with the little hunter dog by his side was reminiscent of cartoon sketches he had seen, regarding tally-ho Englishmen setting out to bag some wildlife. Few could disagree with Moriarty on this, for Barnabas Salmon truly was the epitome of the type of English rural gentleman who had once roamed the countryside of Ireland, and for all they knew might still inhabit certain country areas of England. It wasn't just his attire, but also his tall straight-backed aristocratic bearings combined with the various references he had made to childhood days in that idyllic English village. By all accounts, horse riding, fox hunting and shooting were all part of his heritage. They assumed that it was only the onset of rheumatism that prevented him from maintaining his active participation in country pursuits.

The crowd at the midnight Mass contained all the familiar faces, but there were others whose presence caused a ripple of gossip, and a fair few nudges to be passed along the sturdy wooden benches.

People who had declined to attend Mass for years walked in as if they had never been away, including Connor Meade who had endured a kicked arse courtesy of the priest who had ministered the parish in the 1980's. Ever since that humiliating occasion, Connor had regularly declared to anyone who could be bothered to listen, that he would never set foot in THAT CHURCH again. He turned up, accompanied by his bored looking wife and two children who, between them, demonstrated in perfect unison the wrong time to sit and the wrong time to stand.

Connor Meade was the only son of Pat Meade, a baker and confectioner of some repute. As a teenager, Connor had organised the first youth club in the parish. The parish priest at the time had reluctantly agreed to the idea, but had issued Meade with a number of terms and conditions, one of these being that music was not to be played in the parish hall after nine o'clock in the evening.

The priest had appeared one Friday night, shortly after the music curfew, to find Connor Meade acting the role of DJ, shaking and rolling his head in time to Hot

Chocolate's rendition of "Heaven is in the back seat of my Cadillac." Enraged by the breaking of the "after nine" rule and scandalized by the lyrics of the song, the priest had stormed forward. He had mercilessly scraped the needle over the shameless LP, and consequently brought the music to a screeching halt.

'Get out of here you class of heathens,' he had yelled, 'get out and get back to the holes you have crept out of.' The group of teenagers who, up to that minute, had been admiring Connor's stylish disco unit had immediately scattered like birds that had just caught the eye of a hungry cat, leaving Connor alone to face the angry man in black.

'For goodness sake,' Connor Meade had exclaimed, 'you'll ruin my record.'

'Ruin your record,' the priest had shouted back, almost incandescent with rage, 'you ignorant pup, it's you who is doing the ruining around here; not just to your own black soul but the souls of others as well.' In addition, with that, he had snapped the LP in half across his knee. That was bad enough, but as the broken -hearted Connor had bent down to retrieve the scattered bits of vinyl, the priest had landed a smart kick to his arse bone.

'F-- off with you,' Meade had shouted, and the priest had turned such a deep shade of puce that Meade had seen fit to run for his life.

The upshot was that the priest took possession of Meade's prize possession, the turntable, and refused to give it back until he had received a full and abject apology. Now Connor Meade, as the son of parents who would hear no wrong about their child, refused to offer any apology, and his outraged parents backed him to the hilt. It would have remained a private standoff, but for the staging of the parish amateur dramatic society's rather ironic production of "The Sound of Music."

The priest had announced at Mass that he would not allow the production to go ahead unless he received an apology from a very rude and malcontent young man who was being aided and abetted by parents who should know better. The parish had been divided on the matter. On the one hand, the priest in question was a notable brute who needed taking down a peg or two, but on the other hand, Connor Meade was the epitome of a spoiled brat whose very backside had been crying out to heaven for someone to administer a dose of discipline to it.

In the end, it was decided that too much work had gone into the musical, and so Meade was worked upon and eventually agreed to bite his tongue and apologise. He did so, the priest handed over the keys of the hall and handed back Meade his equipment, and the boy and his parents never darkened the door of the church again.

Yet here he was, some twenty years later, back at midnight Mass. It was rumoured that Salmon was a regular visitor to the Meade household, and apparently after hearing the story he had told Connor that personally, all things considered, he was on the side of the priest. The truth, he had declared was that anyone caught playing such dreadful music, when Iron Maiden and Deep Purple had been available, was simply asking for trouble.

The Meades were not the only ones to create a stir by their presence. Old Bridie Clancy, the Selfish Midget had shuffled into the church just as the Mass had commenced, elbowing her way through the crowd congregated at the door, and glaring at anyone who dared to look sideways at her. She made her way to the bench closest to the altar squeezing a family of six like a concertina as she eased her way onto the edge of the front seat from where she proceeded to glare at the priest in her own indomitable way.

No one had the slightest idea where Father Salmon was going to lead them as he forsook the pulpit in favour of his familiar position in the centre aisle. Most had every expectation that since he was standing in for Father Ryan at the last minute, he would follow the example of the parish priest; remind them that Christmas was a time of goodwill, and extend a brief word of thanks for all the cards and presents delivered to the presbytery. Some, however, eagerly awaited a unique take on the great feast, in the hopes that he would regale them with more tales of his childhood. It was, after all, such a naturally nostalgic time of year, and it was impossible to think that a romantic like Father Salmon could ever view Christmas present as being half as cosy, grand or sentimental, as that of Christmas past.

'My dear people,' he began, 'I would like to relay to you some words from that architect of modern Christmas, Mr Charles Dickens. "Happy, happy Christmas that can win us back the delusion of our childhood days, recall to the old man the pleasure of his youth, and transport the traveller back to his fireside and quiet home."

'I confess to you all that every Christmas I am transported back to my childhood, and you are all aware by now how much emphasis I place on that stage of life.

'And I don't believe for one moment that I am alone in thinking that Christmas invites us unconsciously, and sometimes quite consciously, to look back. One only has to take Christmas cards as an example. Just what is the fixation with scenes of a coach and four dashing through snow-laden fields, or groups of bonneted women and men in tailcoats singing as merrily as thrushes, holding lanterns in one hand and a muffler in the other?

'You see, Christmas invites us not just to look out for others, but to look back into ourselves. We are after all the sum of past experiences.

'Oh, the Christmases of yesterday. Letters had to be written to Father Christmas, in the very best of handwriting of course, and old Jim Crane the gardener was given strict instructions about which holly tree to trim. The dear woman who worked as a daily help and who went by the delightful name of Mrs Honeysuckle, would oversee the decoration of the house, and since it was a very big and rather ornate one - that was no small job, I can tell you.

'Like most young fellows of my generation, I longed for railway sets, and I will never forget the Christmas when Clarissa received a doll that opened and shut its eyes.

'What a great pity it is that we lose the ability to be thrilled and awestruck by the sheer simplicity of a childhood Christmas, because, in a nutshell, from a child's point of view, Christmas is all about giving and receiving gifts, eating and drinking in celebration.

'Remember parents, Christmas teaches children so much about the importance of a heart being in the right place, and in so doing it lays down a blueprint for how to live or, as the case may be, how not to live.

'A young lady once told me that her mother always stressed the importance of a happy romantic courtship. If in the future, dark clouds should overshadow life, the happy days of courtship would remain as a testimony to a time when all seemed to be perfect.

'Christmas is the courtship of our lives, but luckily it is not a once off occasion. Is there anyone here who doesn't sometimes think that life can feel careworn, old and repetitive? There are so many troubles that can beset us. Problems arise at work or with relationships, and we can feel overburdened when the things that are meant to be positives in our lives suddenly become negatives. When that happens, it is easy to imagine that the very earth itself is tired and disillusioned, but then Christmas comes upon us with such feverishness, agility and joviality; bursting with the frenzy of youth, and if we only allow ourselves, we can become truly invigorated.

'I once heard a clergyman describe Christmas as the Disneyfication of Christianity, and by that I suppose he meant it was all rather glitzy, trite and twee. Nothing could be further from the truth.

'In fact the modern pursuit that seems intent upon stripping Christmas of all its fun is, I fear, a rather dangerous one. Much of it starts with good intentions, such as persuading people to donate to charity rather than spend money on sending cards. Now, charity begins at home, but as Christians, we know that it doesn't stay there. What if people decided, en masse, to send no more cards and to cease bothering with decorations, since when all is said and done they are rather wasteful? Oh and since the decorations have gone, why have fairy lights? Don't they look rather trite. Now with the house stripped of all that tack, why go to all the hassle of ordering and cooking a goose or a turkey, when sausages or pasta will do? In that scenario, talk of steaming a plum pudding for hours on end is pure madness.

'Do we not know human nature? If we roll back and roll back, we will eventually meet where the puritans left off. Remember, those are the people who made the baking of mince pies at Christmas an offence. Is there anyone who believes that such killjoy people would donate the cost of Christmas to strangers in the third world? When joy and merriment become things of derision, a mean pragmatism takes their place. Donations to charity would nosedive, because a new era of excessive thrift would encourage the austere to realise just how much they have saved and can pocket for a rainy day. A life lived in gloom can make one spectacularly blind to believing in the possibility of sunshine.

'While I was in England, I stopped off in London to catch my train to Kent and I was shocked at the paucity of Christmas lights and decorations. There wasn't even a Christmas tree at Waterloo station, and although the shops were festooned with stickers urging people to spend, very few actually had decorations. There was one exception. It was a small confectionary shop lit up with fairy lights and festooned with streamers. I watched the fascinated face of a child and I remembered that scene in the film of "Gone with the Wind", when Rhett Butler tells Scarlett O'Hara to watch the burning of Atlanta, so that she can tell her grandchildren that she was there, when that fine city was burnt to the ground.

'Look at the glory of Christmas, protect it and do not ever allow you or yours to be part of the generation that permits it to disappear. Put aside the cynics, and hold on to the joy and merriment for it is what God intended us for, and never underestimate its power for good.

'And one last thing: When the bright lights of Christmas fade, to be replaced by the bleakness of January nights, do not fret about being the perfect family, be a holy one, and perfection will follow in its time, and in its place.'

Chapter Seven

The Boxing Hare

After Women's Little Christmas in January, the temperature plunged to freezing. For a time, ice and snow slowed the pace of the little village further still, as some roads remained blocked, cutting it off to a certain extent, from the world outside.

The heating broke down in the church and, to the amusement of the parishioners, Father Salmon turned up to offer Mass dressed as if he was heading for the Siberian outback. He remained steadfast, despite the cold, inclement weather and continued, undeterred, to visit the housebound, the lonely and some people whom most inhabitants avoided at all costs.

With each Mass, the parish learnt more about their Saxon priest. They discovered that, naturally, as a man who had once been destined for a life in the theatre, he was an avid reader. He loved the works of Tolstoy and Victor Hugo, and was excessively proud of Chesterton, calling him the greatest Englishman that ever lived.

He was also heavily influenced in his theology by the Danish theologian Soren Kierkegaard. Salmon's fascination with Danish writers had started with his childhood infatuation with the fairy tales of Hans Christian Andersen, an infatuation which had never left him. In fact, the older he grew, the more convinced he became that the never-ending appeal of fairy tales was that, for all their wonder and magic, they were rooted in the deep clay of reality.

As he settled into the rhythm of the West Cork countryside and his parishioners conjectured about him, he in turn indulged in various thoughts about them. The one that recurred most frequently was the thought that, for all the stoicism and flint-like faces of the people in the locality, they lived a more ethereal existence than they realized.

He listened one day, completely entranced, to an interview being conducted by the local radio station. A publican from a bar in the village of Droumbally was being questioned about the successful establishment he ran, which had won numerous awards. It was going to be featured in an upcoming BBC programme about the South West of Ireland.

Tom Murphy was the name of the publican, and he owned and ran a large bar and restaurant which overlooked the estuary at its finest point. From all accounts, Murphy had created a masterpiece from very poor material. In the hands of its previous occupants, the bar had disintegrated and had become run-down and ramshackle. No advantage had been taken of its scenic location, and it had offered no enticement such as food or comfortable furnishings to attract tourists and locals alike. The moment Tom Murphy purchased the property he transformed it. A carpenter by trade, he ripped out the interior and began refurbishing it in the style of a comfortable country house. Polished oak floorboards took the place of the stained old matting and large comfortable sofas and leather captain's chairs replaced the tired old wooden stools. To the side of the main bar he built a superb glass conservatory where he housed his specialist seafood restaurant so that diners could fully appreciate the enchanting location. He renamed the premises, calling it The Boxing Hare, and invested in large and colourful artistic signage that caught the iconic image of a hare posed in the boxing position. Inside the main entrance, he invested in a small area which served as an information bureau on the fauna and flora of the entire locality, and from here he presented himself as something of a specialist, a preserver of all that is valuable in the Irish countryside.

Murphy spoke in the interview about his humble origins. He had grown up the youngest of ten children in a house with no running water. He mentioned that it had been a lifelong ambition to combine the two loves of his life, hospitality and the Irish countryside. He said that he wanted to build a destination venue that would attract people from far and wide to excellent wining and dining, and at the same time draw attention to the abundant beauty and splendour of the Irish countryside, which he felt was often neglected in favour of promoting agriculture. As he had spoken, Salmon had found himself being drawn to the story as if he were listening to a fairy tale. The man spoke from the heart and although it was clear he was happy to have made money, he reiterated on several occasions a personal need to champion the gift of nature with which God had blessed the vicinity. Murphy spoke lyrically about the joy of being able to take an early morning stroll and meeting foxes on their way back from a night shift, or witnessing stags standing guard over their young. He declared that he could never tire of the dawn chorus, but that the most spectacular sight of all was to observe, in spring, the spectacle of hares boxing. The imagery had captivated him so much that when it came to renaming the bar there was only one choice, so henceforth the old Sailor bar became known as The Boxing Hare.

Salmon had chuckled throughout the broadcast, recognising a fellow storyteller, and the thought had occurred to him that Tom Murphy might well be in the pay of the tourist board, for the man was a born propagandist.

The interview ended with Murphy recalling the day Brad Pitt and Angelina Jolie had dined at his establishment, a declaration that left the interviewer gobsmacked.

'By God, they were a lovely couple altogether,' Murphy had declared. 'They sat at that table there in the far corner, happy to be acknowledged, and happier still to be left to get on with their meal like two normal folks altogether. When they left, Brad told me that he considered this the finest spot in the whole of Ireland. He said, "We'll be back" and that nowhere could match The Boxing Hare for tranquillity.'

A few weeks later, as Barnabas Salmon happened to be passing The Boxing Hare, he noticed Tom Murphy brushing down the wood decking that surrounded the conservatory restaurant. Murphy was a cheerful looking man with an aura of boundless energy about him. He looked up and acknowledged the priest with a smile and a wave.

'Good morning Mr Murphy,' Salmon called out. 'Is it true you never take a break from hard work?'

'Well Father, I have an image to keep up,' Murphy laughed.

'Yes,' the priest acknowledged. 'A very good one from all accounts, you are a credit to the entire area.' He stopped and stood for a moment, gazing out at the visage of the surrounding estuary with the dark canopy of trees that shaded one side of it, home, no doubt, to the numerous birds Murphy had mentioned. 'You have a grand location here, but there are many who would not have made the use of it that you have done, all praise to you.'

'Yes,' Murphy agreed, leaning on the yard-brush, happy for the opportunity to take a break. 'It is wonderful and I won't deny that it took a great deal of hard work, but it is paying off, thank God.'

'Good news is always grand to hear,' Salmon replied, and as he turned to go, he paused for a moment. 'As a one-time hopeful thespian Tom,' he said, 'I really have to ask you, what were Brad and Angelina really like?'

Tom Murphy threw his head back and laughed. 'I'll tell you the truth Father,' he said, swinging the brush as if it were a golf club. 'I haven't the faintest idea, I never met them.'

'But I heard you telling the chap on the radio about the tranquillity Brad loved so much and….' the priest stopped, and caught Murphy's eye.

'Well Tom Murphy, I'd say you are every bit as sly as those old foxes you meet on their way back from the night shift.'

'To tell you honestly Father, the fox comes to me for lessons in cunning,' Murphy said with a smile, 'but in fairness with regard to Brad and Angelina, there were rumours that they were in the area, but their visit was cut short for some reason.'

'Oh I see,' said Salmon nodding his head. 'So you merely extrapolated what they would have said, if they'd been fortunate enough to have dined with you.'

'I think that is an excellent way of putting it Father,' Murphy agreed.

'Well all I can say,' said the priest preparing to take his leave again, 'is the foxes 'round here have an excellent teacher.'

He took his leave feeling nothing but respect for the publican. The man had been given talents and he was using them. He had elevated the actors concerned, said nothing detrimental about them, but had demonstrated very well that he had the gift of the gab and was not afraid to use it.

He mentioned Murphy to Father Ryan over dinner later that same night, although he did not bring up the visit of Brad and Angelina.

'Murphy took a grand little pub, and lives and works only for the visitor,' Ryan informed him.

'But his pub, and certainly his restaurant have put this place on the map,' Salmon replied.

'Had you ever heard of it before you came here?' Ryan asked belligerently.

'No,' Salmon conceded, 'but then again, I am hardly his target audience am I?'

'It's the jumped up brigade he's after,' Ryan informed Salmon. 'When the Scott family had the place, fishermen could come in without changing their clothes, as could anyone, but now it's restricted to those with the money. Have you seen the prices he charges?'

'No, I have not,' Salmon confessed, 'but time is progress and from what I can see, he has done a service to the area.'

'He has done a service to himself,' Ryan replied.

''And a service for the unemployed,' Salmon argued, 'he must employ upwards of thirty people in the summer months, that has to be a boon.'

'For how long?' Ryan countered, 'and besides, what if every bar in the village decided to turn its back on the local trade, who would serve the local interest then?'

Salmon changed the subject since he could see that the conversation reflected Ryan's mood more than his core beliefs, but later on, he thought over carefully the story told by Murphy to the radio station, and the reaction of the parish priest to the publican's success. He knew that Ryan had the ear of the parish, and was probably in tune with the majority view of Murphy. Sunshine might be in short supply, he thought, but there were no shortage of begrudgers in the region. For people who lived in a place of fairy tale enchantment, they were spectacularly lacking in their ability to appreciate a happy ending. The next time he preached, he did so with Hans Christian Andersen in mind.

'Every person's life is a fairy tale written by God's fingers,' he told the seated congregation at the start of his sermon.

'When I think about the village of my childhood memories, I see a fairy-tale existence. The village church, you know, was mentioned in the Doomsday book of 1086, but its history actually went back to the seventh century. On a clear day, the towers of Canterbury Cathedral could be seen from the church tower. That little church was said to be the last resting place of the shrine of St Augustine, and what became of it after the reformation, nobody knows. The aura of the entire church was one of tranquillity, and while, even then, the numbers who worshipped there were in decline, the churchyard where the faithful from days gone by slept in peace was a reminder of how deep and how far back the roots of faith go.

'Can any of us here today, imagine what it was like to live through the reformation? It is my belief that if, in say the tenth or eleventh century, someone had prophesied about the reformation that was going to turn Europe upside down, they would have been chased out of town for telling stories.

'Sometimes fairy tales are almost overwhelming, either by virtue of their intricacy or sheer simplicity. A lot of very clever people dismiss them purely because they fail to understand them, but it is my personal contention, that the very essence of what makes a fairy tale is at the heart of spiritual growth.

'The forest, for example is a recurring feature of many fairy tales, and in reality we are all, at some time, called upon to enter an unknown forest in the course of life. Like so many fairy tale characters, we are called to face and conquer our innermost fear, be it loss, jealousy or rejection. During our time of turmoil in that dark forest, we live in hope that something sacred and profound will emerge.

'You see, fairy tales differ from fantasy tales because they deal almost exclusively with very mundane, hence very real, human situations. Take the issue of unfairness. Fairy tales are packed with examples of younger brothers or sisters being treated unfairly, or family inheritance going to the wrong people, something that is no rare occurrence in either tales or reality. We can identify with these things, because life shows us all the time that bad things can happen to good people and vice versa. But the beauty that fascinates and attracts children to fairy tales is the realization that the poorly treated hero or heroine always finds restitution. Moreover, it invariably comes about by the intervention of someone who is good. Hope is always curative, and we do well to live in expectation of it.

'Scapegoating is another dominant feature of fairy tales. Snow White is the scapegoat of the wicked queen's obsession with youth; Cinderella is scapegoated for holding a mirror to the ugly sisters. As for poor old Hansel and Gretel, they were blamed for driving their parents into poverty. The unifying factor between all these scapegoated characters is that they must be eliminated or, at the very least, excluded. These scapegoated characters are burdens, and part of the human psyche is to seek relief from burdens, even when they are self-imposed.

'Individuals and groups do it all the time; it goes on in school playgrounds and places of work, and it is not an insignificant vice because, in its own way, scapegoating is what led to the Holocaust. The Jewish people had to be eliminated on a false premise.

'Even in the modern era, where there are so many attractions, children are still drawn to tales that teach them so very much. But if adults have a mind to it, they too can learn from them on a very different level. You see, fairy tales are dynamic. They mirror the process of life with all its fluctuations and eternal moving from darkness into light, the changing seasons and, last but not least, the transformation from weakness into strength. This is true of life; everything changes and nothing can remain the same.

'Consider for one moment your beautiful environment. On the face of it, nothing can change the fact that you have a coastline and hills and valleys, and a sky bursting with stars at night, but even so, nature is always on the move. Erosion and acid rain all make for minuscule changes, often not visible to the naked eye, but it is happening all the same. There are other changes that are much more visual, schools open and close, as do bars and post offices, and indeed churches, and all these changes are part of the life process.

'So you might say, what is the relevance of all this to a Christian? Well the critical thing is the role you play in the fairy tale that is life. Do you see yourself as a witch or a wizard, an evil stepmother or a jealous older brother? Are you the sort of person who will begrudge someone a promotion, even a kind word, yet jump in your car and drive miles to attend the funeral of someone you hardly knew?

'It is often in the capacity of each and every one of us to become the happy ending for someone. Be empathic, and show the inner fairy godmother or inner prince that secretly dwells within you. Bring God into the fairy tale of your life.'

This sermon received a very mixed bag of responses. For some it confirmed what they had long believed, namely that the man had more than a slate missing. Whoever before had heard of adults being influenced by fairy tales? As for others, they sensed that behind all the fluff, the priest was aiming a distinct rebuke at them. It was in their nature to begrudge, and to be told so clearly that their hobby was not benign was a personal insult.

Those who were of a mind to begrudge and criticise were handed a perfect opportunity to vent their spleen when it was announced the following week that Father Salmon was going to England once again to see his "beloved Clarissa." Some priest he was turning out to be, giving ridiculous stories about fairy tales and returning to the UK like a boomerang.

But as always, there was a remnant of people who held true. Those who formed this particular one believed that, by touching on the theme of abandonment and the necessity of hope, Barnabas Salmon had confirmed that they had a priest who was taking religion out of the physical building of the church, and into the realms of real life.

Like the mist Tom Murphy had spoken about on the radio, which descends without warning on the fields and valleys of the village, some felt something of that ethereal spirit in the words spoken by the priest. His disappearance from the parish left them awaiting his return with the same sense of urgency with which one seeks a signpost when lost in an unknown place.

Chapter Eight

The Soldier and the Doctor

Barnabas Salmon returned home from England in a relaxed frame of mind. He relayed to his parishioners the message that Clarissa sent her love and gratitude for all their good wishes, and said that she found the idea of people far away carrying her in their thoughts and prayers to be a sign of exquisite goodness and beauty.

'When I describe the wild Atlantic and the calm tranquillity of the hills and byways, she tells me that, while physically out of sorts - the sheer vitality that is West Cork never fails to rejuvenate her, even through second hand contact.'

The parish faithful learnt, to their surprise, that Clarissa had actually visited Ireland several times over the years and what was more, she had stayed in West Cork on a number of occasions and had even visited the village of Droumbally some years previously. Therefore, when Barnabas described certain things to her, she was able to put them in place and context.

'I tell her, of course, that while the place has physically changed, courtesy of your visiting Tiger, some things are eternal, such as the endless ocean and the warmth of a hospitable heart.'

A few days after his return, Salmon set out to visit the local National school. Some of the children there were looking forward to their first holy communion and he called into the school and watched as they prepared decorations for the church.

The principal of the school was a pragmatic and dynamic, hardworking man by the name of Gerry O'Mahoney who worked ceaselessly for the well-being of the school, earning it an excellent reputation. The atmosphere was lively and radiant with energy, and Salmon felt enormous respect for the driven and capable principal. As the children filed out to play at break time, Barnabas Salmon stayed behind to catch up with the latest news, and O'Mahoney teased Salmon about his holiday.

'I wonder how you put up with meandering about the place here,' the principal said, pushing a cup of tea towards the priest, 'it must be deadly quiet for you after London.'

'Well I only pass through London,' Salmon replied, 'unfortunately there is no way it can be avoided if one wants to get to Kent, but even so, I will admit that there is something rejuvenating about the place with its hustle and bustle.'

'Well England is England I suppose,' O'Mahoney replied, 'this must be one hell of a culture shock to you.'

'You know something Gerry, the English undoubtedly have a strange view of Ireland, but I'll tell you this, the same could be said about the Irish as well. Very often they speak as if the English were a single group, and nothing could be further from the truth,' Salmon said as he dipped a biscuit into his tea. 'For example, Kentish cherry pickers have little in common with steel workers in Sheffield or coal miners in Durham. Some of the ancestors of my parishioners in Kent may well have come to Ireland to plunder it, but equally, some of today's generation have barely heard of the place, and certainly have little or no idea what constitutes the North or the Republic.'

'Are you telling me, Father, that they are ignorant then?'

'Not at all, it is just a fact that people are often only interested in things with which they have a connection, no matter how frail the link might be. I mean, could the average person here tell you, offhand, whereabouts in France you would find Nantes?'

'I follow what you are saying,' O'Mahoney concurred thoughtfully. 'It never fails to irritate me when broad strokes are used to describe any group; it is not a healthy perspective.'

'No, you are absolutely right, but sometimes people do it through lack of knowledge rather than malice,' Salmon replied, replacing his teacup back onto the desk. 'Some years ago, I happened to be in Dublin when Ireland beat Italy in the world cup, and when I returned home, I told my parish all about the great excitement it caused here. Now there was a woman, a lovely person, gentle and refined, a librarian by occupation, so educated enough, and when I told her about the atmosphere in Dublin, she threw her hands in the air and said, "Oh how marvellous, I do so love the Irish, they are such a happy race."'

'Had she ever set foot in the place?' O'Mahoney laughed. 'She'd go home with her delusion in tatters.'

'No, you see the point I want to make Gerry, is that a lot of Irish might take her reaction as an act of English condescension, and nothing could be further from the truth, with that particular woman at any rate. Mind you, she stumped me completely, when she added, "I can just imagine them returning home with happy hearts with their little donkey carts going before them." I sincerely thought she was taking the mickey, but she was being absolutely genuine. The poor woman believed in a storybook image of Ireland.'

'Or perhaps she was just plain stupid,' O'Mahoney offered.

'Whatever she was, Gerry, she certainly wasn't malicious, but I'd doubt many Irish would give her the benefit of the doubt. The English and Irish co-exist alongside each other like an unhappily married couple, oblivious to the real merits and too conscious of the failings of each other. It would take a very clever counsellor to get the party that has most to answer for to even consider the possibility of fault, never mind set about making amends.'

While Father Salmon was in good form and exuded tranquillity, it was becoming apparent that, physically, he was failing. He continued to walk the length and breadth of the parish but at a noticeably slower pace, and whilst getting down on his knees was a challenge, getting off them was positively painful to behold. He looked much older than his mid-sixties, and it was obvious that no matter how privileged his life might once have been, he had encountered the hardship of ill health somewhere along the way. Some parishioners attributed his physical decline to the fact that he was probably paying the price for having played rugby as a younger man, a game that, according to his staunchest critic, the hillbilly Ger O'Reilly, was the preserve of the cream of the country, the rich and thick.

He continued to slowly introduce English customs into the Mass, greeting parishioners at the door, and encouraging the children of the parish to sit together to form their own liturgical group. His masses were longer than was usual, and people who had spent time in England confirmed that it was the norm for English priests to make a meal out of the sacrifice.

'It is the Protestant influence,' Sam Horan, a parishioner who never ventured beyond the church porch declared one night in White's bar when the English priest cropped up as a subject of conversation. 'Protestant's don't have so many rules and regulations concerning saints and whatnot, so they tend to go for drawing their services out like, to make an impact.'

'Personally, I've always found English Catholics to be more devout,' responded his companion, John Walsh, a timid looking man who worked as a carpenter.

'He sounds like a Protestant to me,' James White, the publican remarked. 'That church he talked about from his childhood village; that definitely would have been Protestant.'

'It would have been Catholic before the Reformation,' Walsh suggested.

'Yeah, well Salmon was hardly a lad at the time of the Reformation was he?' White returned. 'The truth is, he talks about a Protestant society with all the emphasis being on order and moneyed people; you have to wonder what made him become a priest.'

'Well, he obviously comes from the upper echelons of English society, going by that accent of his,' Walsh again suggested, 'and Catholics would be few enough amongst them, it must lead to a siege-like mentality when you're part of a minority, so fair play to the man.'

Whenever the rural gentleman was discussed, the nature of the conversation always flowed along similar lines to the one the one that had been held in White's bar. The priest aroused a mixture of responses from his congregation, but this did not deter people from going to Mass on Saturday evenings. In fact, listening to the priest made many feel that a story was unfolding, and that a punch line would ultimately be delivered at a given time and place.

The fact that the man was relentlessly easy-going and cheerful, yet never compromised himself by trying to ingratiate himself amongst a people who, while outwardly hospitable, were internally insular, only served to make some more willing to get to know him.

Attuned to their instinctive nature and take on social topics, Salmon did not hesitate to use the gospel readings as a torch to shed some light on what he took to be a pressing issue of the day.

On the occasion when he discussed the gospel concerning the healing of the ten lepers, he broke with tradition. Instead of focusing on the ungrateful nature of the nine who never returned to give thanks, he emphasised the isolation sufferers of that terrible disease would have endured at the time of Christ. Within seconds, everyone knew he was taking the opportunity to face head on the elephant in the room of Irish society.

'It is a terrible thought to know that a loved one is suffering,' he began, 'and even worse to know that they are alone and far from you. I take great comfort from the fact that so many of you retain Clarissa in your prayers, and I know that the fact that she is remembered by people who do not even know her, gives her great comfort.

'I am of course greatly saddened by her poor physical health, but the greatest tragedy for me is that she has no faith whatsoever. She married in the Church of England, and no doubt one day, hopefully in the distant future, she will be buried alongside her deceased husband according to the rites and rituals of that persuasion. I believe her lack of faith robs her of much comfort.

'That splendid church which I told you about, which dominated the village of my childhood was of course a Protestant one. There is a great irony, I think, in that Catholicism, which is the oldest denomination in Britain, is generally practised in modern churches, while its offshoot makes its home in the original buildings.

'I might well be wrong, since no one can possibly know the heart or mind of another, but I have a suspicion that Clarissa's lack of faith owes something to her perception that many people who claim to know Christ, often cannot abide each other. G.K. Chesterton put it succinctly when he stated that the Bible tells us to love our neighbours and our enemies, probably because, generally speaking, they are the same people.

'You see, for all their talk about being grounded and factual, atheists are often very idealistic people. For starters, they think everything was made by nothing, which is truly quite remarkable. They also, naively, think that perfection should come easily to a Christian. They say, "You are the ones that extol mercy and forgiveness, so go ahead and practise what you preach". Clarissa has a great respect for Catholicism, and yet she remains convinced that it is based on superstition. Like Voltaire, her take is that superstition is to religion what astrology is to astronomy, the mad daughter of a wise mother. Unfortunately, these two daughters, namely superstition and astrology, have been around for a long time, and although reason calls for them to be rejected, there can be no denying that it is very hard to cut off and cast adrift a relation. Atheists I think have a habit of throwing babies out with the bath water, and my beloved Clarissa is no exception.

'While I was across with Clarissa, I took the opportunity to call on a few old friends, and I read a good many newspapers, something I am not in the habit of doing when in Ireland. I came across two articles in the English press that stuck in my mind. One concerned the death of an old soldier, and the second was a comment made by an atheist doctor.

'The old soldier died alone, and the shocking thing is that not one person attended his funeral. People expressed a great deal of sadness at this news story. The consensus was; how terrible that a man who fought for his country should be buried without even the company of a dog at his funeral. My mind turned instantly to babies and bathwater.

'Why, I wondered, were so many people preoccupied with the fact that no one attended the funeral of a man's remains? The big issue, surely, is the loneliness and alienation that same poor man had endured, possibly for most of his life. Loneliness, my dear people, is a silent killer. It is all around us, and there is a tendency for people to think it is confined to squalid bedsits in sleazy cities, but nothing could be further from the truth.

'What though is loneliness? Is it a fear of life? Is it inevitable, considering that one is born, and will die alone? Greater philosophers than I long ago determined that we live forwards and remember backwards. Therein perhaps resides a key, for memory can often be the gateway that leads to lonesome thoughts. If we look back on our life with a searchlight, we run the risk of remembering too starkly past grief and missed opportunities, and find ourselves perversely choosing alienation. Suddenly, all the unfairness, slights, mischief and prejudice that we have encountered or dished out to others, is illuminated too brilliantly by the beam of the searchlight. And our response might cause us to either withdraw into ourselves or unintentionally send a signal out to others that makes us brittle in the face of human interaction.

'Yet as believers, we have to move forward; we are seekers, but ultimately what we seek is not to be found, not in this life at any rate.

'Loneliness is like the mist that descends on the village from the sea. It can find its way into everything; no one is immune to it, but some are more strategically placed to attract it. For some, it is physically possible to move out of its direction. Take for example young people who feel cut adrift from their community. They might leave and go to Dublin, or even move abroad and start anew, but that option of upping sticks is not open to everyone. The elderly living in the back of beyond or the neglected spouse, they cannot just rise up and go. We need to be keepers of each other. This society is changing, perhaps faster than any other comparable one in Europe, and the question is, are you and your neighbour ready for it?

'The second article in the English press that caught my attention was the assertion by an atheist doctor that he would like the God in which Christians believe to take an inspection of a cancer ward. "Ask him: what do you think of your handiwork?" he advised. It struck me as a very stupid comment for an educated person to make, and while it might infuriate the man, I couldn't help wondering what he would make of Chesterton's assertion that if there were no God, there would be no atheists.

'But I digress, because the point I want to leave you with is that there is a meeting place between the burial of the old soldier and the doctor's assertion, and it is this: without God there is no point. Why visit the sick, the old or the lonely? It might be a nice thing to do, but ultimately, in the grand scheme of things, it is pointless.

'Watch yourselves, watch each other, all boats rise in the tide and so they fall when the tide goes out, which it always must do, eventually.'

Chapter Nine

Choices, Choices, Choices

When Father Salmon first arrived in the village of Droumbally, the so-called Tiger boom of the Irish economy had been at its height, but it had been obvious to his eyes that the prosperity he witnessed was a novelty rather than an ingrained habit. He had ministered for most of his priesthood in plush and established areas of Kent, Surrey and south London where the dwellings, apart from sprawling council estates, had, in the main, been a comfortable mix of Edwardian, Victorian and post war structures.

The mushrooming of large and elaborate houses that were being built, not just in the vicinity of Droumbally village but also, from what he could gather from the media, throughout the length and breadth of Ireland, both intrigued and fascinated him.

It had occurred to him that he was watching a modern day gold rush in full flow. Money had just been discovered, and the rush was on to buy cars, big ones especially, with four-by-fours being the speciality. Along with the cars came the holidays, with New York being a favoured shopping destination. There was a general free-for-all to spend, spend, and spend again. He was not, in any sense, puritanical, and the sight of so much activity had filled him with pleasure, for nothing warms the heart like the sight of happy people doing what they love best.

However, he came upon it all as an outsider and therefore, from the start, his natural position was that of an onlooker rather than participant. Much as he didn't want to acknowledge it, the obsession with money and the spending of it eventually made him feel distinctly uneasy. He was reminded of Kant's observation that "it is easy to be immature." The people he had moved amongst to serve were stoic, land-based people who, for generations, had been shaped by the fierceness of the environment surrounding them, but the fruits of the booming economy were undeniably sweet and enticing.

It was not the urge to spend that concerned him, for that was a normal phenomenon. No, it was the urgency to depart from old measured ways of thinking and doing. He noted that even the most stoic of people were being tempted into abandoning the notion of thinking for themselves. It appeared to Salmon that politicians, auctioneers, media personalities and economists were doing the thinking, the advising and the analysing. A collective responsibility had been handed over to them with no reflection and no analysis of the reliability of that trust. He took issue with Father Ryan's gruff condemnation of people with two children buying six bedroomed houses when they themselves had been reared with six siblings in two bedroomed houses.

It was a hackneyed expression that flew in the face of reason. Progress was progress, what could be wrong with people wanting a better life for themselves and their children?

Salmon could find no fault with that desire *per se*, but what he did query was the undesirable by-product of that desire. The quality of life for many people was improving, but it was at the dictate of a consumerist led society that proliferated itself by crowning Choice as its king.

Choice was all very well, Salmon thought, but it was infinite, and the problem with infinity, as someone once said, is that there is just too much of it. What concerned him was the notion of choice for choice's sake. Choice was a noun that was increasingly being hijacked by big business in particular. By becoming a slave to it, Ireland would have to abandon its rural pace and attitudes because choice always brought in its wake the spectre of missed opportunities. Many choices invariably led to compromises having to be made. To choose one thing over another usually involved an element of sacrifice, but the more choices one has available, the more sacrifices one might have to make, and how wearing that could sometimes be.

The love of money was, he observed, like a kind of cholesterol spreading through the arteries of the country, choking its very heart.

It was with some dismay that the priest saw a planning notice in the paper concerning Sam Dunne's farm. He immediately set out to visit the old man who was distinctly worried about the implications for himself.

'They hardly have the time of day for me now,' he told the priest. 'All they can talk about is planning, surveys and architects, where is it all going to end?

'I don't know Sam,' Salmon replied in a rare tone of seriousness, 'life can go anywhere or nowhere'.

'Well, you may be certain sure that it is on the road to nowhere right now,' the old man complained, 'did you ever have the like of this carry on in England?'

'To an extent yes,' Salmon replied. 'The housing boom of the 1980's in England was frenzied, and it caused a great deal of damage when it went into freefall. However it did not take long for people to forget, and I suppose that is a good thing, otherwise we'd all be still be in caves remembering the man who got eaten by the mammoth when he ventured off the beaten track.'

'Ah, so you do think this bubble will burst.'

'Who knows Sam; I was merely recalling a boom in England that unfortunately ended in a bust. I hope and pray it will be different here.'

'Don't they say the English never remember while us Irish never forget?' the old man replied with a small smile, 'you are breaking with tradition.'

'I rather think that is changing,' Salmon replied quietly. 'I am of the impression now that the Irish only want to forget, they are smothering the past like one might quench a fire by throwing a blanket over it until not one ember remains. The general consensus is that it was all bad.'

'And much of it was,' Sam Dunne replied tiredly. 'I remember my poor mother, God rest her, she worked night and day on this farm with no electricity and no running water except for the damp; it was a tough existence.'

'Oh believe me Sam, I am no champion of the past, much of it was terrible and thank God it has gone, but it is simplistic to dismiss it out of hand, because not all of it was bad. I am of the impression that the old adage will change, and it will be Ireland that forgets and England who remembers.'

'What put that idea into your head?'

'Well, on the last few occasions when I was over,' Salmon replied. 'I was struck by a growing nostalgia regarding the Second World War, and a tendency to view the generation who fought and lived through it as selfless and heroic icons. It is good to see, but sad as well, because many believe it cannot be repeated. What point is there in remembering a golden age if there is no appetite to replicate it?'

'What does this generation know at all? As far as Anne and Noel are concerned I am as much use as the cat, perhaps even less since at least she catches mice.'

'But are they involving you at all?' the priest asked. 'Are you being asked or just being told about their plans Sam? Surely the property is still morally yours, even if you have signed it over.'

'And where would that get me,' the old man demanded. 'You can afford disputes when you are young, but the moment you become reliant on others, well it is a different story. Didn't Christ himself say that when you get old, they will put a belt around you and take you where you'd rather not go? It's all about what they want, what they decide or choose to do, they don't include me.'

Salmon did not ask the old man to expand upon his fear, for he knew instinctively what it was. Sam feared that any attempt to seek redress, and so upset the apple cart, might well result in him being abandoned to the nursing home in the town. Sam Dunne's fate depended largely on how far his family had bought into the new mantra of 'break the hold of the past' which included shared experiences.

In Barnabas Salmon's opinion, the new society that was emerging had no blueprint for guidance. Young and old were being thrown in at the deep end and having to move fast and thoughtlessly to keep pace with the changes. The greatest tragedy was that the stalwarts of traditional guidance were being revealed every day to have feet of clay and were no longer to be trusted. It was his suspicion that the hierarchy of the church believed that a crash was coming, and that it was going to be of both a spiritual and economic nature. Rather than make an attempt at being some kind of buttress, it had made the choice to retreat.

The society was in a state of flux, but as an outsider, and an English one at that, he felt he was in no position to offer an opinion. His heart would have been warmed though, if he knew that many parishioners would have been dismayed if they had known that he still saw himself as an outsider. With each passing day, they warmed to the rural gentleman and appreciated his tact and his concern. With Father Ryan it was a very different scenario, for he had always made it very clear that his priestly mission was to attend to the sins of the parish, all else was the business of living and had nothing to do with him.

The uniqueness of Father Salmon's preaching wasn't just in what he said, but the manner in which he said it. Just as many individuals become convinced that the eyes of Mona Lisa follow them specifically when her picture adorns a wall, many parishioners left the Droumbally church convinced that Father Barnabas Salmon was speaking uniquely to them.

One such person was the newly married teacher Eddie Moran. Eddie had thought long and hard about Father Salmon's sermon regarding marriage. Most especially, he had dwelled upon the phrase "quality over quantity." He had almost convinced himself that the priest had been addressing him personally, and would sanction and perhaps even recommend, Eddie settling for quality.

He arrived unexpectedly one night at the presbytery, and asked Father Salmon if he could spare a few minutes. Father Salmon showed Eddie into the rather tired looking study and the few minutes quickly turned into a few hours. The young man spoke gently and honestly about his situation. In summary, he declared that he had known his wife too long. There was no passion and, prior to the marriage, he had been too cowardly to call it off.

'If Father, I had realised that what I feel for Carolyn is nothing more than friendship, I might have had the integrity to at least have postponed the wedding.'

'Would you?' the priest had queried, 'or would you have done your utmost to drive her away and so save yourself the hassle of responsibility?'

Eddie had been dismayed at the apparent lack of sympathy, and the priest had silently noticed this, so he focused the searchlight more acutely on Eddie.

'Tell me Eddie,' he said, 'if say a few weeks or a few days before the wedding, Carolyn had told you that she wanted to break it off or that she was unsure and wanted more time to think, would you have been grateful or hurt?'

'I don't know Father,' the man replied after a lengthy silence. 'If I am honest, I only truly felt the way I do now after the ceremony was over, but now when I think about it, I see that we had no courtship, not like other people seem to do anyway. We met at school and we went to the same places. Our families know each other, and even though Carolyn's father is not over keen on me, even that provided grit, in a way, to polish it all off. Fundamentally, it just feels so past tense.'

'When did you decide to get married, Eddie?' the priest asked, watching the man carefully.

'We went to school together, like I just told you; we went to college, I went to Limerick and she went to Dublin. It doesn't feel to me as if I ever made a decision, it was just an understanding that suddenly became a reality.'

'But surely there was a period of official engagement,' the priest persisted.

The young man got up and walked to the window, where he stood gazing into the darkness. Turning around to look at the priest, he said. 'I bought the engagement ring five years ago, we set the date then.'

'And how did you spend the five years?'

'How does anyone spend time,' Eddie replied a little irritably. 'We went on holidays, we had a house built on the land Carolyn's father gave us, we lived.'

'Actually Eddie I beg to differ,' Father Salmon spoke just a little sharply. 'You lived more in the expectation of living, which is exactly what you are doing now.'

The man returned to his seat opposite the priest. 'I really don't get your drift Father; do you understand what I am saying? I am in despair, I feel my life has ended and I can't let it happen.'

'So what do you intend to do Eddie? Save your life and destroy that of your wife, her family and your family as well? I think you are being very selective about what you remember of my sermon regarding marriage. Do you recall me saying that marriage is never just about two people?'

'For me Father, you put your finger on it when you quoted Chekov, what was it, if you're frightened of loneliness do not marry. I am lonely Father. I am married to someone I have nothing in common with. I feel like a condemned man. There are so many places I could go, so much I could do, but I feel as if I am chained.'

'Chekov, for your information Eddie, was the son of a despotic father, so there is little wonder he considered marriage a lonely option; it almost certainly was for Chekov's mother. He was speaking about his own experience, not yours. As for you, my advice would be to work backwards from where you are now and retrieve your marriage. The pair of you put the cart before the horse, you built a house, built careers, went on holiday, and by so doing you lived back to front.'

The priest paused since he knew his words were falling on stony ground. He also suspected that Eddie was probably in the process of kicking himself for having opened his heart to someone who was not shocked by its contents.

'It is up to you Eddie, but it seems to me that you view your wedding vows as a life imprisonment, and by doing so you are burying your living soul. Either you came to see me for reassurance that it is legitimate to walk away from your marriage or you came for help in how to save it. Which is it?'

The man refused to meet the eyes of the priest, instead he kept his eyes fixed firmly on the floor, looking grim faced and perplexed.

'If you want to save your marriage Eddie, you'll have to work hard at it. Make a resolve to get to know each other again and strip away the security that led you into a trap. Some years ago, a parishioner in London gave me a budgie; I never figured if it was meant as an insult. Anyway, sometimes I used to let it out of its cage on a night and the blighter would fly to a carved apex on top of the dresser where it was impossible to reach. I would have to leave it there, but when I came down in the morning it would still be there chirping away. I realised eventually that if I left the cage door open it would probably fly back in of its own accord. So I did just that and when I came down the following morning, there were feathers all over the cage. The housekeeper's cat had eaten it. The moral of the story Eddie, is that the very place where you think safety and security can be found is often no more than a trap. Talk to Carolyn honestly, and if she is game for it, sell up, move away and rely on each other. Experience the coldness of exile together, live dangerously and put yourselves in God's hands.'

Silence greeted the priest and eventually Eddie got to his feet. 'Thank you for your time Father,' he said a little stiffly, and took his departure.

Father Salmon saw him to the door and returned to the window where he could just about make out the outline of the young man as he made his way down the path. He was sad to see the man look so dejected, but he understood the reason for it. He had made the perennial mistake of thinking that happiness automatically follows on the heels of getting what you want. Eddie Moran had been asked to deprive himself of his heart's treasure, which in this case was freedom, and like countless others, Eddie wanted to be able to have his cake and eat it. He was the victim of a culture that said such a thing was possible, even though countless generations who had gone before him had evidence to the contrary.

Chapter Ten

The Blossoming of Bridie

It will come as no surprise to learn that the rural gentleman became a frequent visitor to the abode of the selfish midget. Many of the local people were quite shocked, for Bridie Clancy had a strong long-standing aversion to both priests and nuns.

'Scavenging crows,' she called them, 'out to pick and tear apart the lambs from the sheepfold.'

For all that Bridie was such a terrifying spectre to her neighbours, it was actually quite easy for an unwary stranger to be beguiled by her for, from afar, she looked small and benign. It was only when one had the misfortune to become embroiled in a close up confrontation with her that the full extent of her bitter features became obvious. While her husband had been alive, she had acquired a reputation for being both a street and a house devil. The few contemporaries of Bridie who still survived in the area remembered her as the only child of small time farmers, both of whom had been getting on in years by the time Bridie had been born. From all accounts, she had been a fine looking young woman with a pretty face and an enviable mane of dark hair that had been her pride and joy. She had left the area at a very young age to work in one of the big houses on the outskirts of Cork city, a practice that was common at the time. Rumours of a scandal, which had involved Bridie, had seeped back to her native village, but nothing had ever been substantiated - possibly because if it had been, something would had to have been done about it. Even so, given the cultural climate of that age, rumours had been enough to bring vengeance on swift wings and, for a good many years, Bridie had been banished to the city. After leaving the big house, she had eventually found work in a factory.

She had faded from memory until, by chance, she met her future husband while he was delivering fish to the shops and restaurants in the city. At the age of forty, she married and returned to the area of her childhood, and the rows and ructions in which she and Charlie engaged became legendary. People recalled Charlie telling a passing farmer one day, as he sat ducked beneath a hedge that he failed to understand why the good Lord had blessed Bridie with such an accurate aim. Neither party had elicited much sympathy. "God made them and the devil matched them," had been the dismissive attitude of most. No man in his right mind would put up with a harridan like Bridie, and no sensible woman would have tolerated the shambolic Charlie.

With Charlie long gone, Bridie now lived alone but she furnished many a tale told in the bars and shops of Droumbally. A popular one was how she had sent a self-important politician fleeing in fear of his life when he had been foolish enough to canvass for her vote. She had seen him off with a barrage of language which one of the more demure neighbours had transcribed as being something about 'bucking frolics' accompanied by a shower of rotten spuds and apples, one of which had knocked the jaunty looking cap clean off the politicians head.

In the past, some had sought to put out the hand of friendship to her, and she had taken it and used it to her advantage before thoroughly biting it.

A handyman by the name of Tim Dooley was her nearest neighbour, and in the past he had mended Bridie's fence on a few occasions, unblocked her drains and even seen to her electrics following a severe storm. When snow and ice had made her path dangerous, he had cleared it, or sent one of his young sons to do the job as an exercise in overcoming fear of wild dogs. For all his efforts, he had never received even so much as a word of thanks, but when, without planning permission, he had put a small window in the rear roof of his house she had promptly reported him to the planning department. They had no option but to pursue a case against Dooley, because she hounded them with threats. In the end, at great expense in terms of both time and money, Dooley had to remove the window. He never darkened her property again, but when he met her by chance one night on the road, he told her that she was a right old bitch of a woman and Bridie promptly reported him to the guards for harassment. To satisfy her, the guards came and harassed Tom. No one in the area could afford to step out of line for she kept a beady, watchful eye on everything. All dogs in that particular vicinity of the village were licensed, and nobody indulged in illegal burning. She was feared and loathed in equal measure, even by the guards whom she bombarded with complaints, which they were legally bound to investigate.

It was therefore not surprising that people warned Father Salmon to tread very delicately around this particular parishioner. When she had made an appearance at his first Christmas midnight Mass, most were of the opinion that she had merely come with the aim of sniffing out fresh meat to torment.

Clancy's neighbours were anxious to protect the priest from his own foolishness. They felt certain that, like the evil troll to be found in fairy tales, she was only waiting her moment to lure him into complacency, before launching a full-scale attack.

'Father, it is not in my nature to speak ill about anyone, least of all an elderly lady,' Maeve Brennan said to him one day as she passed the priest out on the road that led to Clancy's house. 'But I urge you to take care with Bridie, even though I know it is difficult for a priest to be choosy about whom he visits.'

Salmon commanded his dog to sit, and turned to face Maeve. He thought that she was like a ray of sunlight with her tranquil ready smile that was still hovering about her eyes even though she was gearing herself up to speak seriously. He knew her from the village shop; she had been friendly to him since the very day he had arrived.

'My dear, I do not doubt your honourable intentions for one moment, but people do tend to speak of Bridie as if she were an Alsatian rather than a little old lady.'

'To be honest Father, I'd rather face a hungry Alsatian than Bridie Clancy. She has caused immense trouble for a lot of people and we'd be failing in our duty if we did not warn you.'

He looked thoughtfully down at his little dog, Wolf, who was tugging at the lead, and then, turning to look at Maeve again, he said. 'Do you personally know much about Bridie, Maeve? Does anyone have a handle on how or why she became so estranged from everyone?'

'I have no idea Father,' Maeve replied. 'My mother's mother knew her vaguely when she was young. She always said Bridie had been normal enough at school, but something happened and everything changed. She never said what it was, but things were different back then, a lot was brushed under the carpet, but there was definitely a hint of some scandal.'

The priest had looked thoughtful as Maeve had spoken, and when she had finished he had shaken his head sadly and had said quietly. 'Do you know Maeve, I think a life lived free of scandal can often be a very poor one. I imagine when Christ died there was no shortage of stories flying about the place concerning the things he did, and the people with whom he associated; the Pharisees would have had a ball.'

Salmon did not make anyone privy as to how he became an acceptable visitor to Bridie Clancy, but he became more than an acceptable one. He became a frequent one and very soon, the sight of the priest with his little dog trotting by his side became a common one along the road that lead to Clancy's house.

The change did not happen overnight; it fact it was so gradual that few thought to attribute it to Father Salmon, but slowly and steadily Bridie Clancy became a less fearsome character. She no longer patrolled the road outside her cottage like a dog scenting for a fight, but as Jim Brady, the door-to-door fish salesman put it. 'She no longer looks for a fight, but I reckon she'd still be up for one, given a chance.'

She attended Mass more regularly on a Saturday night, turning up late and walking to the front of the church, oblivious to the disruption she caused, and often leaving early, shuffling along the aisle ready to challenge anyone who dared to look at her. On a few occasions, Bridie had been at the front of the church before realising that it was Father Ryan, and not Father Salmon, who was celebrating Mass. When this happened, she promptly turned on her heel and made her way out, muttering as she went. Ryan, rattling through the Mass at the speed of light, spouting platitudes and endless notices riled her. She would not take a lesson on life from someone who didn't have one.

Chapter Eleven

The Seesaw Always Comes Down

Salmon's ability to fascinate his congregation did not diminish with the passing of time. The illness of his sister Clarissa continued to necessitate his disappearance from the parish as he went back to England from time to time to visit her. He always returned replenished, with new stories with which he entertained the parish, and wry observations that both intrigued and delighted.

The congregation learnt on one such occasion that Clarissa was fluent in both French and German, and was a consummate musician, playing both the piano and violin. Her husband, like her father, had been a high-ranking civil servant, and after his death, she had returned to the village of her childhood. Like Barnabas, she also remembered her childhood with affection and nostalgia. The regular attenders of the Saturday evening Mass grew to feel as if they really knew Clarissa. They knew the games she had played as a child, the foods she had disliked, and that, unlike Barnabas, she had never participated in country sports, always choosing to side with the red fox over the hounds.

'The great charm of the English countryside,' Salmon told his parishioners one night, not long after his return from his visit to Clarissa, 'is that it embodies order, sobriety and custom. I feel certain that if you could picture the village of my childhood memory, you would understand why both Clarissa and I felt so very sheltered. There was the church, of course, in all its splendour, and on one side of the village green there were the labourer's cottages, while at the other end of the scale were the great houses of the landed gentry. The memories of childhood days in the countryside are a rich tapestry of many wondrous things, and animals, be they mice, cats or horses, certainly have a large part to play in that picture. As you all know, I have become very attached to my little dog, Wolf, who was given to me by a kind -hearted parishioner. Whenever I see him running out to greet me, I am reminded of an epitaph that apparently marks a grave in Maryland. "Major: Born a dog, died a gentleman."

'All animals have their place in God's world, but the creature that fascinates me almost more than any other is the cuckoo bird.

'I was talking to a lady recently who had just turned ninety, and she told me how, in the Ireland of her youth, the cuckoo was welcomed as the harbinger of spring. The old people of Kent in the 1950's always looked forward to hearing the cuckoo as well. Many believed it meant they would live to see another year. I cannot help wondering, though, if they would have remained so enamoured with the creature if they had known the rather ribald association between the word cuckoo and cuckold.

'It was generally believed, in the Elizabethan, era that a cuckolded husband had to be someone who was a bit slow on the uptake, and this link lingers even to today when we refer to someone who is a bit dim as being cuckoo.

'If you look at it logically though, the cuckoo bird is far from stupid. It spends the best weeks of the year in warm climes and long before humans thought of nannies and crèches, it perfected the art of handing the drudgery of rearing its own over to others. This fine bird, which was once common even in the boroughs surrounding London, is now a rarity, and from what I can deduce, it is not thriving in Ireland either.'

For a moment, the congregation began to wonder if it was a sermon they were listening to, or a speech for a Green Party convention. But just as their interest was beginning to wane, Barnabas Salmon gently manoeuvred his sermon back into the comfortable zone of childhood reminiscence, and his parishioners eagerly tuned back into him, for he was a master storyteller. As they listened, a new image of an ancient foe began to emerge, for he was describing an England with which they were not familiar. They knew, by heart, all about the brutality of the English in Ireland and the uncouthness of characters in certain soap operas. For many, however, it came as something of a surprise to learn that the English at home could live such a charmed existence. However, just as they began to relax into what they thought was an unfolding story; Barnabas Salmon quite suddenly took the sermon on an altogether much sharper tangent.

'During my ministry in England, and indeed during my latest visit there, I came across a lot of cuckoos, Irish ones actually. I am referring of course to the men and women who left the villages they loved in much the same way Clarissa and I love the village of our childhood. These people left Ireland in the 40's, 50's and 60's. Many came to England in search of a better life and the sad truth is, many never found it.

'Some entered a new form of slavery with long hours and low pay, isolated from all that is familiar. Many endured horrific living conditions and this, along with loneliness, drove some to drink, so fuelling the reputation of the drunken Irish. A hand to mouth existence became the lot of many, mainly due to wicked employers, most of them fellow countrymen who never paid the stamp that would have given them a semblance of security. These were people who so longed to be home amongst their own that they never took the steps necessary to become settled in England; but how their contributions kept the home fires burning. Did you know that Irish men in Britain are much more likely to be single, divorced or widowed than the average Briton? Or that twenty percent of Irish pensioners in the UK live alone?

'While visiting Clarissa in hospital, I chanced upon an elderly man sitting, looking very forlorn. He was from county Kerry and had left Ireland in the 1940's at the age of sixteen. He had spent a lifetime in the unskilled sector of the construction industry, and now, at the end of his days, he is alone and his life will end without recognition. He cannot afford to come home. He is not an isolated example either. As a priest, and so privy to unbridled tongues, I know that on the streets of London and many other towns and cities in the UK, scores of Irish men and women are to be found alienated and abandoned.

'People in the past left Ireland for many reasons. You can choose to believe the hype of some politicians and churchmen, who like to paint a picture of people who left Ireland solely to better their economic outlook or for the chance of some adventure. No doubt, some did have itchy feet to see the world, and undoubtedly, many left to fund a better life for themselves and their families. But there were significant numbers, especially amongst women, who were driven out by abuse, violence and menace, and there they remain, out of sight and out of mind.

'The tide was out when these people left Ireland and now it is back in full flow, but they remain a people set apart. They feel abandoned and neglected. They and their offspring figure in the current imagination as "plastic paddies." What an arrogant, ugly insult coined by the very people who benefited from the sacrifice of others. There are stories out there that would break the hardest of hearts, and a collective wall of silence prevents them from being heard.'

A hush descended on the church. Even those who had not been paying particular attention became aware of unease, for the tone of the priest sounded harsh and almost accusatory.

'Charity begins at home, but it does not remain there. How ironic and how bitter a pill it must have been for that Kerry man to listen to a toff like me, tell him that I live in Ireland, and that I am made welcome, while he, who sent money back to build the state, no longer feels wanted.

'Britain has an enormous debt to the Irish workforce who left their homes and came to build their roads, staff their schools and their hospitals. Equally, many in Ireland are indebted to those same people who went to the UK in order to send money to support those remaining at home. Nature never forgets. The long-term prosperity of this country is in jeopardy, if a debt of honour is not repaid.

'Right now in your community there are people in need of understanding, people who have been served a grievous wrong who are rendered incapable of reaching out because rejection fells the dignity of a human more swiftly than an axe fells a tree. And across the water this very night, old men and, indeed, old women from beautiful communities such as this one, on the doorstep of the wild Atlantic, are living a life of rejection. And yet, there was a time when their contributions were the cornerstone of many a family.

'Support your emigrant brothers and sisters with your prayers, and make good your intention to always welcome the stranger, for Christ often appears in disguise. The day will come, when your young will leave again, for the seesaw always comes down.'

It was very difficult for some parishioners to dismiss the words of Father Salmon's 'cuckoo' sermon out of hand, although some did try to temper it by saying he had obviously been motivated by a harrowing personal revelation. Others comforted themselves with the notion that the sermon was merely a sign that he felt guilty for having the good fortune to live somewhere he loved being.

However, for those who always-paid attention to what Barnabas Salmon said, it was becoming clearer with the passing of every season that for all his outward jollity and sense of fun, loneliness, alienation and abandonment were recurrent themes that ran through all his sermons. They also began to believe that the priest deliberately engineered a sense of randomness to his sermons, because the hidden reality was that, for all his apparent casualness, there was a real structure to the mission of Father Barnabas Salmon.

Chapter Twelve

Undermined

Occasionally, Father Ryan would visit Slattery's bar in the village, where he would sit on a high stool at the heavy wooden bar, surrounded by his school-day friends and companions, and discuss, at length, the merits and possibilities of various racing greyhounds. As someone born and reared in the area, he was on familiar terms with the vast majority of people in the vicinity. discerning gambler interests, knew something about their occupations, and when the fancy took him, he would drop into Slattery's bar, which was the favoured saloon of the more discerning gambler.

Ryan was not a devout priest, but he was a faithful one. He had no handle whatsoever on Barnabas Salmon and was mature enough to admit to a faint feeling of jealousy on account of the sheer amount of interest that the rural gentleman provoked. On a personal level, he thought the English priest spoke claptrap; a lot of nonsense and trite tripe about his childhood and his youthful ambitions, quoting authors whom most of the parish didn't know and wouldn't want to know even if they lived several lifetimes.

Unfortunately, Salmon tended to bring out in Ryan a faint rekindling of an inferiority complex that had dogged him for most of his life, even though he had learnt to hide it, as he had grown older. He had always been inordinately proud of the fact that his family were referred to as 'big' farmers, and was well aware that his family had been better off than those of his contemporaries. As a child, he had attended school better fed, better dressed, and better prepared. Since teachers are always more inclined to favour such children in preference to those sporting running green noses and hacking coughs, Ryan had excelled academically. Quite naturally, the young Donal Ryan had attributed his scholarly success to innate intelligence, but when he had gone on to the seminary, the shock of no longer being a big fish in a small pond had both confused and dismayed him. Like a strutting Lilliputian who stumbles across Gulliver, he had realised that he, and indeed his background, were not, after all, as good as it gets.

Now, on the onset of old age, he was saddled with the company of a priest a few years his junior who had enjoyed a childhood that made Ryan's background look paltry by comparison. There was however, something that managed to make Ryan still feel quite superior; Salmon was younger than he was by a few years, and yet looked considerably older. As a man who had always been quite vain about his appearance, this gave Ryan a lot of pleasure. There was something else as well; Barnabas Salmon, by his own admission, had been a sickly specimen of a child, given to a whole range of illnesses and ailments, while Ryan, on the other hand, had been a sturdy child full of rude good health. There was a certain degree of satisfaction to be had from knowing that there are compensations when one cannot have it all.

Ryan did not share his parishioners' delight with Salmon's clear enunciated tone and diction. Sometimes, when he heard the loud almost booming voice greeting a visitor or answering the telephone, he felt almost incandescent with rage. Why couldn't the man tone it down? Or better still, discover the art of whispering. Another thing that irritated him was Salmon's obsession with books. Hardly a week went by when one did not arrive in the post for Salmon, always something new about Christian philosophy, much of it American drivel. The bookcase in the study that had once just housed traditional religious tomes concerning the catechism was now stuffed with the works of Kierkegaard, Dostoyevsky, Anna Akhmatova, Tolstoy, Victor Hugo, and to Ryan's absolute amusement, Hans Christian Andersen. Now, the latter did not surprise Ryan in the slightest, for he had long been convinced that Salmon had rats in the attic.

However, the single biggest issue about Salmon that disconcerted Ryan and left him feeling bewildered and, if he was truthful with himself, a little hurt, was that while Salmon opened his heart to his congregation, he never opened it to Ryan. On several occasions, Ryan had tried to lead the way by talking about his own background. He regaled Salmon with tales of how, as a child, he had detested having anything to do with cows, and how this had forced him into thinking up many creative ways to avoid being drafted whenever help was required with milking or cleaning out the byres. But Salmon refused to take the bait, and never discussed his childhood with Ryan. Sometimes he spoke about various parishes he had served in London, and occasionally even about past parishioners who had made an impression on him, for good or ill, but he never discussed his early life.

And yet when he did speak, Father Ryan always felt his own world shrinking, and although he knew that Salmon was only responding to an enquiry of his, he felt a pulse of inferiority stir within, and for this he was inclined to blame Salmon rather than himself.

Salmon never ventured into any of the village bars, for he felt strongly that these were not his domain, and if he were to step into one, all normal conversation would immediately cease, rendering the visit pointless. He met most parishioners by chance, walking through the village or along the beach. Those who wanted to talk would engage, and often walk alongside him. Sometimes, they simply took the opportunity to ask him to call on them. Intuitively, many parishioners knew that little dialogue flowed between the two priests. In subjects that involved feuding between families or neighbours, parishioners were inclined to seek the opinion and counsel of the priest who had no divided loyalties.

There was relief in not having to call to the presbytery, or make a telephone call and have to think of ways to sidestep Ryan without hurting his feelings. Everyone knew that the English priest was bound to be out on the road, so it was just a matter of tracking him down. His faithful companion, Wolf, presented a ready opportunity to waylay the priest, as people stopped on a pretext of fussing over the small animal before engaging with its master.

It was on one such occasion that Father Salmon came across a young woman walking on the beach, accompanied by two children. It was immediately apparent that the woman was the mother, for all three of them had startling blonde hair, and even from a distance, an aura of wealth and elegance radiated from the trio. The moment the two little girls spotted Wolf, they left their mother's side and ran across to Salmon and the dog.

'Oh, he is a darling,' said one of the little girls. 'Oh he is just so sweet.'

Her voice was English, and Salmon recognised it instantly as being from the plush south, Surrey most likely. Close up, the affluence of the children became more apparent in terms of their dress, accent and confidence.

'Does he bite?' the second child asked, patting the dog's head before Salmon could reply.

'Only biscuits and ham bones,' he said, smiling at her, 'he is generally a well behaved fellow and if he wasn't, he would be grounded.'

The dog, who was a well-handled creature and used to the attention of people, basked in the fuss being lavished on him by the two children. He sat up on his hind legs, rolled on his back and displayed every trick in his repertoire to keep the attention focused.

Salmon, seeing that the two girls were virtually identical felt safe in asking, 'Are you twins?'

'Yes,' replied one of the children. 'I am older than her by ten whole minutes.'

'My,' he replied, 'so you have a younger sister and you,' he said, turning to the other child, 'have an older sister.'

'What is the dog's name?' asked the older child. It was apparent that the one who had arrived first had bagged most of the confidence.

'His name is Wolf,' Salmon replied. 'Wolf by name and wolf by nature, or so he likes to think when he sees cats and rabbits.'

The woman began to approach the priest and the children, but she stopped, keeping a distance from them all.

'Good morning,' Salmon said to her, doffing his cap as he spoke, 'I am afraid this dog is a terrible attention seeker.'

The woman nodded but did not return his greeting.

'Mummy can we get a dog like this one?' the second child, who had hardly spoken until this point, asked, running up to her mother to demonstrate the veracity of her request.

The mother shook her head slowly and appeared to look beyond the three people and the dog.

'Do you live near here?' asked the dominant child, 'Do you often come to this beach? Will we be able to see Wolf again?'

The priest laughed. 'Yes I live here and I do come to this beach when the weather allows, so I am sure Wolf will be happy to see you again.'

He turned to acknowledge the mother, to apologise for the disruption to her walk, and saw that while she was staring at him, she clearly wasn't seeing him. He looked at her more thoroughly, she was an exceptionally good-looking woman, tall and slim with shoulder length blonde hair. She was simply and elegantly dressed in well-cut jeans with a long loose top. Her thoughts were clearly far away, so he took the opportunity to look at her again, this time focusing more clearly on her. She looked familiar, and he wondered where he had seen her before. He had a good memory for faces but he could not, at this moment recall from where he might have known her. His mind began a thorough search, but it reached a blank; he could not remember where he had seen this woman before, but he felt quite certain that she was not a complete stranger.

She moved her head slightly, and the movement seemed to jolt her out of her daydream and in an instant, she noticed the man searching her face.

'Come on,' she said to her children, 'we have to get home.'

The children took no notice of their mother for they were entirely captivated by the dog, which, at this stage, was being held like a baby by the eldest of the twins. The dog wore a big silly grin on its face as one child hugged it, and the other stroked it within an inch of its life. He nestled his head against the child's shoulder, tossing it occasionally and delivering a series of licks with its pink tongue onto the cheeks of each child as if determined to share his affection equally.

'My dears, your mother is calling you,' Salmon said to the children, 'and Wolf and I must go home.'

He could see that the woman was agitated, and he didn't want to be party to her distress.

'Oh, just another minute,' the children begged in unison and Salmon looked to the mother for direction.

As he looked into the woman's face, the sight that met him left him feeling quite physically shaken. The good-looking face was quite wretched in its despair, and as she turned her eyes to meet his, he saw nothing but despondency in them. The woman looked soulless and distraught, and he knew that she was submerged in pure desperate grief. It was not in Salmon's nature to barge into the life of others. He ministered to people who signalled by word or deed that his counsel was sought, because of all the gifts God had bestowed amongst mankind, Salmon rated the gift of free will above all others. He was tolerant and ecumenical almost to a fault, but the sight of evangelical preachers, parading about with placards, declaiming dodgy theology that declared death would always be followed by unfavourable judgement both enraged and offended him. It was he believed, a strategy that was as far removed from the spirit of the Christian gospel as it was possible to get, employed by people ignorant to the idea of a susceptible stranger.

Yet there was something about this woman's face, which pulled at his conscience, and he could not walk by without acknowledging in some small way, that he was aware of her misery.

'I am a priest,' he told her quietly. 'I live at the presbytery in the village.'

She turned and fixed her spiritless eyes on him. 'Really,' she replied, in a tone of such disinterest that he could have been informing her of anything, ranging from being a reincarnation of Napoleon to telling her yesterday's weather forecast.

'Yes,' he replied, 'it is hard to believe considering my apparel, but it is the truth.'

'Truth,' she repeated, as if it were the only word she had caught. 'What is truth?'

With that, she turned her back to him and began to walk away. He whistled and Wolf broke free from the arms of the child.

'I think you had better go with your mother,' he told the children. 'I am sure we will meet again.'

Back once again at the presbytery, Salmon fed the dog, and secured him to the long line of wire that gave the dog a measure of freedom while keeping him secure, and walked slowly into the house, to the sitting room where he usually gave thought to upcoming sermons.

He was troubled by his encounter with the family on the beach, and convinced that he had seen the woman somewhere once before. It was not recollection of her face that bothered him the most; it was her look of complete and utter despair. He felt a sense of powerlessness. The woman had quoted the words of Pontius Pilate, but even before she had opened her mouth he had instinctively known that she was every bit as confused and troubled as that far off Roman administrator undoubtedly would have been the day he had washed his hands over the spilling of innocent blood.

'Many years ago,' he told the congregation at the next Saturday night Mass, 'I heard a very informative programme on the radio about missing people. A variety of people spoke about husbands, wives, sons and daughters, brothers and sisters; people who had suddenly taken it into their heads to disappear.

'The one thing that bound each story to the next was the resolute insistence that the disappearances had occurred without warning. One woman said of her husband, "He got up, ate breakfast and left the house at the normal time and I never saw him again. There was no indication that anything was wrong."

'One minute someone was there, the next they were gone.

'I found myself wondering, was there really no warning, or was it more likely that warnings had not been heeded, and that was actually the reason behind someone choosing to disappear?

'As Christians, we believe that despair is the ultimate sin. After all, it was the suicide of Judas rather than his betrayal of Jesus that dammed him, since it demonstrated how little faith he had in the mercy of Christ. The others disciples did pretty despicable things as well, they deserted him, dozed off when he most needed them, and even denied him, but they all remained open to his mercy, and so avoided the pit of despair.

'Be sure, this is not a rush to judgement on anyone who has died by their own hand. No one knows the mind of another anymore than he or she knows the mind of God.

'The words of today's gospel always strike deep into my heart, and I grieve for some stoic staunch atheists who live unaware of their existence and deeper meaning.

'Surely life means more than food and the body more than clothing.

'Christ posits the question, "Can any of you by worrying, add a single hour to your life?"

'But what I want to talk about today, are the people who do not seek to add to their allotted span of life, but rather seek to end the life they have been given. To return so to speak.'

At this point Salmon paused, aware of the unrelenting hush that had descended on the congregation. There was not one person present who could recall a time when they had ever heard a priest speak openly about the subject of suicide. It was a taboo subject. Hints and allusions had been made to it, often shrouded in platitudes that were as clear as wooden windows, but no priest had ever used the term suicide from that altar. A shared thought occurred to many, did Father Salmon have a proper grasp on just how delicate and proscribed this subject truly was?

It was a topic that had recently dominated the news. There had been the sudden death of a well-known personality, a horrific case of murder suicide, and even in the locality, there had been two deaths, one of a young man in a car crash, and the other concerning that of an elderly bachelor farmer, that were regarded as suspicious, to say the least.

'Albert Camus was a French philosopher and writer,' the priest continued. 'He said something that encapsulates a trait of which I fear I might be guilty. He said, "some people talk in their sleep, lecturers talk while other people sleep."

'I have no wish to bore you or send you to sleep, on the contrary I want to captivate you and urge you to think deeply. I am perturbed at the way suicide is being addressed, because all the hype and sensation is leading us to believe that the issue is being dealt with, and I am afraid that just is not true. The media deal with the finality. We learn that the body of so-and-so was found or discovered, but scant attention is being paid to why. Oh, we have plenty of cheap sensationalism that often subtly tries to lay blame on others, perhaps in the cynical hope of developing another storyline, hence the revelations of immensely personal details such as failed relationships or difficulties at school or at work. At the other extreme, we have mass outpourings of sentimentality that almost imply something heroic or inevitable about the deed. Neither reaction offers any reflection on the deeper meaning of why.

'I mentioned Camus because he had some very interesting thoughts on this subject. He was an atheist who was baptised a Catholic, and who was killed instantly in a car crash. My own very personal contention is that had he lived, he would have come back to his faith, but that is a subject for another time and place.

'There was one word in particular which he used about the 'flight from light,' which struck me to the heart: "undermined."

'Undermined! Repeat it to yourself. Do you, like me, feel a dragging sensation even as you speak it? The very heaviness of the word, and the idea that it expresses, strips away what it is to be human. We are not dealing with a new invention, because the issue has been around since time immemorial. There is an added poignancy however; when in good times, so many people feel driven to do something so bad, and by bad, I mean something that is caused by misery and goes on to create even darker misery.

'What is the tipping balance? Does it vary from person to person, or is there a kernel of truth that links, if not all, at least a great many cases together?

'My own conjecture, or philosophy if you will, is similar to that of Camus. Suicide comes from spiritual ill health and stems from a deep confusion about man's place in the scheme of things. The Roman Catholic Church is often vilified for its perceived historical efforts in days gone by to keep the bible out of the hands of ordinary people, but it wasn't altogether just about a power grab on behalf of the clergy. Knowledge is important, but so is the use of it. It is not enough to know the mechanics of how to pilot a plane, knowledge about a great many disciplines must accompany it, and if it doesn't, catastrophe will follow.

'We can access vast information about the planets in the solar system and indeed about life miles under the sea, but without the ability to truly understand where we are in relation to them, such basic knowledge can lead to a feeling that a small, individual life is insignificant in comparison to the vastness of time and space. We are undermined.

'What a despairing thought; that we are of no significance. It is an invitation to give up. What is the point of salt if it has no flavour?

'Not one of us is immune, and not one of us can truly know how a look or a word might drive someone closer to the edge or encourage a retreat from it. Like its incestuous relation loneliness, despair is frequently a silent killer.

'The Danish philosopher and theologian Søren Kierkegaard remarked that the greatest most petrifying hazard any of us can face, is to lose oneself, and the truly terrifying thing is that this loss can occur so quietly that no one in the world even notices it at all. Other losses, be they money or relationships, come to the world's attention, but the loss of self happens silently and with disastrous consequences. To lose someone we love is traumatic, but as believers in Christ we believe that our mortal end is only the beginning; but to lose ourselves, well, the loss of self is irretrievable since with it goes the ability to care.

'Listen, and take to heart, and heed the words of tonight's gospel. "Your heavenly father knows your needs." Faith is rooted in reason, but reason, to make sense, must be rooted in faith. As Catholics, we are open to the wonders of science and technology, and anyone who accuses us of not being open is talking nonsense, because the very world we inhabit is run by these concepts. But be wary of scientists and technologists who are a closed book when it comes to spiritual possibility, because they most certainly cannot be party to the full story.

'Trust, and give others a reason to trust as well.

'It is easy to forget that life is brief, and easier still to forget that, for all its turmoil and anxiety, there is nothing more fascinating than life.

'"Happiness is not only a hope but is, in some strange manner a memory, we are all "kings in exile." So, said the great Chesterton. Think on those words of his, and this sermon of mine might make more sense.'

Chapter Thirteen

The Spectre of David Copperfield

The parish considered Father Salmon's sermon on suicide to be highly controversial. Many were stunned by his words. Yet for all the shock expressed, most parishioners believed that he had been brave to speak out. In fulfilment of Salmon's dedicated wish that religion should escape the physical confines of the church, the subject matter of his sermon was discussed vigorously in the homes and bars of the parish.

Danny Moran, a long distance lorry driver who worked for a major food distributor hailed Father Salmon as a hero.

'I'm telling you,' he told White the barman, who had just insisted that the priest was playing a risky hand, 'You fellows who stay cooped up around here don't know the half of it. Suicide is becoming nothing less than a curse upon this country, and it can't be swept under the carpet much longer.'

'In fairness Danny,' White had replied. 'I can't see a whole lot of point in talking about it, anyone at Mass is hardly likely to be tempted into doing it are they, and it was insensitive, given he can't know the personal histories of many in this area.'

'Oh, you mean the O'Sullivan girl doing away with herself some years back?' Danny replied.

'Well yes, but God knows she is not the only one, there are others, and you have to think what their families will make about Salmon carping on about it all.'

'They'll make a bloody deal of sense out of it,' Con Murphy, a dairy farmer, interrupted. 'They'll think if somebody years ago had the balls to say it like it is, things might well have been different.'

'You are missing the point Con,' White replied. 'If someone is intent on doing away with themselves, there is nothing you or me or even a smart talking priest can do about it.'

'I think Con has it about right,' remarked the smooth quiet tones of Bart Kinsella, a tall mild looking man who farmed a good acreage of land on the outskirts of the parish. Kinsella had himself once suffered a bout of notoriety following his wedding to the daughter of a well -known social outcast some years previously. The village had waited in vain for his marriage to the volatile Kate Ann to prove as disastrous as his father and indeed the parish priest at the time, had warned him it would be. Happily, they had all been proved wrong. The marriage of the Kinsella's was, without doubt, one of the closest and most contented the village had ever witnessed.

'The point Father Salmon made tonight is a valid one,' Kinsella continued in his mild voice, 'there has to be more neighbourly observation and less heaping the load onto backs that are already brought low.'

'And what would you propose Father Kinsella?' asked the cynical barman, 'would you have us all snooping on one another.'

'Some do that already,' Con Murphy pointed out with a grin at Kinsella, 'why when I forget what I had for breakfast there is no shortage of people who can remind me, but in fairness it has nothing to do with snooping, it means having a bit of integrity and looking out for others.'

'Exactly,' Kinsella agreed, 'no one can have anything but admiration for someone who lightens the load of another, and as the man said, doing nothing for others is the undoing of ourselves.'

It wasn't just the parishioners and wider community who were fired into discussion and reflection by the sermon on suicide. Father Ryan felt duty bound to question Father Salmon about the wisdom of opening up this particular can of worms.

'I take your point very seriously Donal,' Salmon said to his superior. 'It is a delicate issue but unfortunately it is not one that is going to take itself away.'

'Have you any idea what suicide represents to people in Ireland, to this locality in particular?' Ryan persisted. 'This isn't England; we are not dealing with a large fragmented society where lots of people live an estranged existence and so remain unaffected by the actions of each other.'

'I am quite aware that suicide has a different connotation in Irish society,' Salmon replied in a conciliatory yet not apologetic tone, 'but for all the outcry and recriminations, very little analysis about the precipitating factors seems to be going on. Despair is as much a taboo subject in secular society as it is in the church, although I have a suspicion that it will overwhelm the church itself sooner than later.'

Ryan grunted in contempt. 'I half wonder if it would be as well for the church to cut out all the sympathy, and go back to the days of burying them in un-consecrated ground.'

Salmon shook his head. 'Such a threat only harms the family. The church of "hate the sin and kick the arse of the sinner" punished the living by burying their dead as outcasts. One day the ghosts of those wronged will rise and we will all have to face the music.'

'You do know that it is generally assumed that the Mitchell fellow who died over in Kildowey crashed his car on purpose don't you?' the parish priest asked, deliberately ignoring Salmon's observation.

'Yes,' Salmon replied. 'I had heard about that, he was on my mind when I gave the sermon.'

'Could anyone have prevented it?'

'Who can say,' Salmon replied tiredly, 'but the point is, none of us must slip into thinking that such things are inevitable, rather we have to start acting as if they are possible to avert.'

Ryan remained silent.

'Being English in rural West Cork,' Salmon spoke quietly, 'is a double edged knife. I can see how it must irritate to have an outsider speaking on issues that run deep in small communities, yet on the other hand, a sympathetic outsider can offer another perspective.'

Ryan got up and walked over to the dresser where he uncorked a brandy bottle and poured two huge measures into two brandy glasses. Walking back, he handed one to Salmon and sat down opposite him.

'So, would you impose a bit of British law and order on us all then,' he spoke a little churlishly.

'No need to old boy,' Salmon replied, rising to the innuendo. 'You are doing a fine job of it yourselves; the day will surely come when the Irish will retreat to England in search of a more laid back way of life.'

Ryan sipped at his brandy and sank further back into his chair.

'Hell will freeze over first,' he replied.

'Then the devil must be stockpiling icebergs as we speak,' Salmon replied. 'Last week, the morning after the Healy wedding, guards breathalysed several of the guests as they made their way back to attend Sunday Mass.'

'And?'

'And? Well it is just another example of how the country is becoming clinically sanitised. Would you like some more? How about the government ruling that there is to be no smoking in privately owned establishments, and no children in bars, even though, for generations, sensible people trusted them more than babysitters.

And what about the persistent adverts on the radio telling parents what to feed their children and when to throw food away, the list could go on. The best people to ask are some of the cuckoos who came back searching for the world they left behind.'

Ryan flashed an almost contemptuous look at Salmon before replying in a slightly heated voice: 'I suppose it is quite de rigeur for England to do such things because it is civilised, but Ireland must be kept wild and romantic so the Brits and Germans can come and feel superior?'

Salmon laughed a big hearty laugh that riled Ryan even further. 'Superior, what a very strange word. The Brits and the Germans don't feel superior because they are rule bound; they feel superior because of their size, much like bullies often do. The Brits and the Germans come to Ireland and they love it because they recognise something that has been lost in their own backyard, an age of innocence disappearing, and nobody grieves the loss of innocence more than the debauched.'

Ryan shook his head and a look of melancholy fell upon him as he silently reflected that there might be some truth to what Salmon was saying.

'I know you will think I am as daft as a brush,' Salmon continued, 'but recently I was reading some Dickens and a thought occurred to me. There is actually a great similarity between the history of modern Ireland and the tale of David Copperfield, which incidentally, was written against the backdrop of a great social change, namely the industrial revolution. A whole different class and set of people such as manufacturers and mine owners suddenly became very, very rich.'

'Rather like the developers and auctioneers here today,' Ryan replied gruffly, 'they certainly seem to be on the hogs back.'

'Absolutely,' Salmon agreed, 'and now, as in Dickens' time, a new power house has emerged, but in both cases the gap between rich and poor widened rather than narrowed.'

'Hmm,' Ryan concurred. 'No one can deny that a revolution of sorts is going on here, and where it will all end God alone only knows.'

'But the similarity is more than just the background,' Salmon continued. 'David Copperfield himself embodies the story of Ireland, he endured tyranny at the hands of a brute, poverty, and isolation, but, crucially, he never lost his sense of self and he remained sympathetic to the underdog.'

'And is that where you would have Ireland, the kind hearted underdog of Europe?' Ryan replied sarcastically.

'David did not remain an underdog,' Salmon said reflectively. 'He did remain virtuous and so attracted the attention of the dashing villain Steerforth because, as I said already, degenerates love wholesomeness. The mistake David made was a very human one, he sought the approval of a flatterer; and in terms of an Ireland and Copperfield analogy, I rather think Steerforth is Europe.'

'I think there might be something in what you say,' Ryan acknowledged, 'but a country has to progress and I suppose we have to follow the path well-trodden.'

'That is government talk,' Salmon replied dismissively. 'Is there any progress worth having if the by-product causes its citizens to despise what they are? Eventually politicians retire to count their pensions and from a position of safety, they ruminate on what has been lost, as if they had nothing to do with it. Meanwhile, what becomes of the old fellows living in the back of beyond?'

'You tell me,' Ryan replied, quite taken aback the vehemence of Salmon's speech.

'Very well then,' Salmon replied, as if he had been waiting permission to speak. 'Those old fellows, who spent a life time working, are being degraded into objects of pity and derision, because in this utopia of plenty they can still be satisfied by a few pints shared in the company of a few pals. The term "rural isolation" has been demeaned, it is bandied about like yuppie, or nimby was in the UK. It has become meaningless because no one wants to look into the heart of it...'

'Well, I wouldn't want to meet Donie Reilly tanked up and driving home at eighty miles per hour,' Ryan replied.

'No one in their right mind would either,' Salmon replied, 'but the reality is that most of the old fellows, if left to it, would drive home after a pint or two at ten miles per hour. The nature of modern discourse, however, is to always talk in extremes; hence we hear of thirteen year-old mothers and sixty year-old ones as well.'

A companionable silence fell and was eventually broken by Salmon.

'Talking of mothers, I met a woman on the beach during the week.'

'You'll get yourself talked about,' Ryan remarked drily, 'but you must be used to that by now.'

'Oh I am,' Salmon replied humorously, 'famous for fifteen minutes how will I handle it? No, I met a woman with two young children, two little girls about the age of seven or eight. The poor thing looked wretched, absolutely lost. She has played on my mind since.'

'I have no idea who she could be,' Ryan replied, before catching himself and saying, 'mind you the school over at Dauros enrolled two children for an Easter start. A family has moved into one of the holiday homes up by Slattery's old place. They are English apparently, but the father is from up the country, Meath or Westmeath, I can't remember which.'

'There was no man with the family I met' Salmon replied thoughtfully. 'I truly hope and pray all is well with them.'

Chapter Fourteen

I'm with Nietzsche

Father Ryan's information was absolutely spot on. The family Father Salmon had met on the beach were the very ones who had recently moved into the area.

They were an affluent family from Surrey, and the father who, Ryan had surmised, was from Meath, had taken a sabbatical from his firm in the UK to join a research team at a pharmaceutical company near Cork city. He was rarely to be seen, since he left for work early in the morning, and did not return until much later in the evening. The two little girls, who were called Ianthe and Flora, attended the village school and had, from all accounts, settled very happily there. Most of these details became known through the friends of the children, who took seeds of information home. From there, the seeds were then dispersed more widely by parents who scattered grains of gossip thereby harvesting in turn, more to bring to the table of intrigue. Very little was known about the mother, other than that her name was Fuchsia, and that she had originally hailed from Kent.

Some conjectured as to whether or not there was any possibility that Father Salmon and Fuchsia Delaney might know each other, unaware that Kent was a very large and sprawling county, rather than a village or town. The family did not attend church, although the children were registered at the school as being Catholic.

Salmon occasionally saw the children as they played in the schoolyard, and they instantly recognised Wolf and were eager to renew their acquaintance with him. He came across their mother again quite by chance after paying a visit to Bridie Clancy, or as the village still preferred to call her, the selfish midget. Bridie had suffered a fall and was unable to walk to the village, so the priest made a point of calling on her more frequently than usual. She had been allocated a home help in the form of Alice Tobin and it was from her that the rest of the village learned that, in the company of the rural gentleman, Bridie Clancy could actually act quite civilized. She was less brittle and appeared more at peace with herself.

Alice Tobin could not resist teasing Father Salmon on account of this apparent transformation which nobody, probably with the exception of the priest, believed was permanent. 'You will be getting a following Father,' she said, 'before we know it you'll be known as Saint Barnabas, the wonder maker, untier of knots and you'll have your very own litany.'

Father Salmon had smiled at her and said he hoped he would be consulted on the illustration of any leaflets if they made it to publication and had quietly taken his leave. Instead of returning to the presbytery as he had planned, however, he had taken a detour and headed for the beach, thinking the dog might be grateful for the extra run. It was there he met Fuchsia Delaney again.

She was walking along the seashore dressed as simply as the first time he had seen her. The dog, inquisitive and certain as ever of his own charm, approached her, but here it met with resistance. The woman stared resolutely ahead, ignoring the animal and, after a while, the dog gave her up as a lost cause.

Before coming to West Cork, Barnabas Salmon would never have considered himself as a dog lover. He had taken the runt pup off the O'Haras hands, more to relieve them of a burden than to satisfy a personal need. Within days, however, he had realised that the dog was a Godsend, a real asset in enabling him to get to know people and he had steadily grown incredibly fond of the animal. Even so, he was not blind to the dog's ability to cause aggravation, and rejection of Wolf by others did not break his heart.

He glanced at the woman's profile and the more he looked, the more convinced he became that he had definitely seen her before. The same aura of despair drifted over from her and stripped of the company of her children, she cut an altogether more lonesome figure. Once again, he felt compelled to reach out to her.

'What glorious weather it is,' he remarked, keeping a distance from her so allowing her the possibility of accepting his conversation as a greeting, rather than an invitation to discuss.

'Yes,' she replied after a pause, 'it is very pleasant.'

He put out his hand and said, 'I am Barnabas Salmon, a very rare specimen, an English priest in Ireland.'

She hesitated for a moment but a natural grace and charm urged her to take the proffered hand.

'Hello Father,' she spoke quietly in her fine, precisely modulated voice, 'if it makes you feel any better you look like a local to me. I am Fuchsia Delaney.'

The name, like her face, struck deep into his memory. He knew beyond doubt now that he had most definitely heard that name before. She looked into his face and saw the struggle for recognition, and immediately and quite sharply she withdrew her hand away. Salmon now felt an overriding sense of curiosity, who was she? He felt certain that she was not a former parishioner. Could she, he wondered, be a model or some kind of celebrity? Everything about her spoke of professional beauty; her speech, her deportment, who was she and did she expect to be recognised?

'Ah yes,' he spoke casually, 'Father Ryan, the parish priest, told me that a new family had moved into the area. Are your daughters settling happily into the school, it must be a huge change for them?'

She did not answer for she was in a state of agitation, having seen the look of recognition that had flashed upon the face of the priest the moment he had heard her name.

'Do forgive me for intruding upon you,' he said, anxious to break the unbearable silence, 'but I feel certain that I have seen you before.'

'Well you haven't,' she replied starkly. 'I'm with Nietzsche. God is dead and so I have no need of church.'

'My dear I sincerely apologise if I have upset you,' Salmon replied. 'I am so sorry to have spoilt your solitude,' he bowed his head slightly, as only a rural gentleman could do without looking like a character from a pantomime, and began to walk away. He had walked perhaps five or so metres when he heard her call.

'Father, please wait a moment.' He turned and looked kindly at her.

'I heard someone say you are from Kent,' she said quietly.

'Is that where you hail from?' he asked in a soft voice. 'Perhaps you have heard tales of my childhood days in a little village near Canterbury.'

'Yes, I am from Kent originally,' she told him, 'only I am from the coast, a little further south east from your area.'

'Well south of the Medway makes you a Maid of Kent I believe, rather than a Kentish Maid which is for those born on the wrong side of the river.' He laughed good-naturedly, but she did not respond to his humour.

'You probably saw my face in a newspaper,' she said in a flat tone that seemed to suggest that she felt a certain game was up.

'Please do not read anything into my flimsy recognition of you,' he told her quietly in an altogether different voice to the one with which he usually addressed his parishioners. 'Most priests have a tendency to develop a good memory; it is all part of our training. I am sincerely none the wiser as to whom you are.'

'Sometimes, I feel as if I will never know what it is to be free again,' she replied as if responding to a personal question and Salmon responded as if there was nothing amiss about her response.

'Did you ever really know what it was like in the past?' he asked her quietly.

'Probably not.'

'I am at the presbytery,' he said, 'come and see me if you ever need to talk to someone.' He knew beyond doubt now that the woman was deeply troubled, but he was wary of railroading her into parting with a confidence. It was a desire to give her space, not disinterest that made him begin to walk away once again, but the moment he moved to turn his back, her face, pitiful in its bleakness, moved him to speak again.

'Tell me dear,' he said softly, for even though the sun was shining, her face held the countenance of winter upon it. 'What is it that ails you so badly?'

'I killed my baby, Father.'

At that precise moment, Wolf, bored with the beach, appeared as if from nowhere, and began barking and snapping at the heels of the priest as if to remind his master of his presence. In an instant Salmon quite forgot his fondness for the animal and sincerely wished it a million miles away.

He was shocked at the revelation that the woman had made. He had known from the moment he had set eyes on her that she was a traumatised person, but nothing in her demeanour had prepared him for this confession.

He picked up a stone and hurled it into the distance hoping the dog would play his part and chase after it but it didn't, instead it persisted, yapping first at his feet and then at the feet of the woman. She took no heed of it, but as Salmon watched her, he saw tears running down her face, and if there was one thing that could reduce Salmon himself to tears; it was the sight of them on the face of another. He searched in the inside pocket of his jacket, and pulled out a tissue which she used to wipe her eyes.

'Will it help to talk to me?' he said, courteously taking the tissue from her, and giving her a fresh one to use instead. 'I mean really talk, not here on the beach with a noisy dog and restless sea.'

She nodded her head and he deftly slipped the lead back on the dog. She silently fell into step beside him, and together with the yapping dog, they made their way back to the presbytery.

Chapter Fifteen

A World Full of Miss Havishams

That was the first of several visits Fuchsia Delaney was to make to Father Salmon. In the course of them, he learnt that her eight-week-old baby son had been killed when the car she had been driving had struck another vehicle. He had listened carefully to what the woman told him, and as her story unfolded, he saw that her grief and despair were compounded by a travesty of betrayal and denial on the part of those closest to her. He deduced more from what she omitted rather than from what she said, including that her husband was both austere and impassive, and once again Salmon found himself thinking that the so-called virtue of stoicism was highly overrated.

'Life would be easier, bearable even, if he pointed the finger and blamed me,' she said to Salmon one night as she sat opposite him in the little study at the back of the presbytery.

'Does he blame anyone?' Salmon asked, 'The other driver, or God even?'

'The only person he blames,' she said slowly, 'is himself. I often think he has ruined his life because of me. He should never have married me.'

This particular conversation was slightly at variance with how she usually spoke, for in all the discussions she had engaged in with the priest, she had never made any accusation or criticism against her husband. However, given the scale and nature of the tragedy combined with the woman's apprehensive words, Salmon summoned all the experience he had gained over the years and pieced together an image of a cold and indifferent man.

'When I first saw you on the beach,' he said gently, 'together with your two lovely little girls, some words from the book of Joel immediately sprang to my mind: the sun and moon are darkened and the stars have withdrawn their shining.'

She sighed and shrugged her shoulders. 'Does it ever occur to you that humans have suffered since the start of the world?' she said quietly. 'Think of all the grief that has been endured through the years, way even before Christ was born. People felt like Joel did over two thousand years ago, and yet the same sentiments are being expressed today. It is almost as if no progress has been made.'

She stopped and then turned to say something, but overcome with emotion, she remained silent.

'Tell me,' he said softly, 'what is the story behind your name? I have never met anyone called Fuchsia before, is there a West Cork connection?'

An oppressive silence filled the room, and the woman stared at her hands, which lay limply in her lap.

He knew she was debating the wisdom of enlightening him any further.

'My father came from West Cork,' she said eventually, 'he came from a village just a few miles from here. I never really knew him.'

'Unfortunately,' the priest said sadly, 'that is something a lot of people say about their fathers.'

'Yes,' she agreed, 'I could never get to know mine because I was illegitimate. I still do not know if he abandoned us or if my mother abandoned him. Now they are both dead, I doubt I'll ever find out.'

Her words had an impact on the priest and he remained silent, looking thoughtfully into the middle distance. As he listened to her speak, he grew to realise that the death of her baby was not the only burden she was shouldering.

'The truth is, Father,' she said, turning her gaze upon him. 'I am struggling to maintain a semblance of interest in this life. I cannot reason with it, I do not understand it and I can no longer be bothered with it.'

She did not speak as an actress, though her words were almost theatrical in their intensity and delivery. Salmon had heard more melodrama in the voices of people enquiring about Mass times than he had detected in hers.

'And now your tiny child has gone, you can no longer curtail the despair,' he spoke as if delivering a fact rather than an observation, and she nodded her head in relief that he understood her.

'You know Fuchsia, I rather think some intuition drew you to West Cork,' he told her, 'and by that I mean it was not a rationally thought out move. I suspect there were other places you could have gone to, other places perhaps your husband and his family would have preferred you to have gone.'

'Yes,' she said, 'you are absolutely right. Killian was unhappy at the idea of coming here, but I had to come, and now I am here, I no longer understand what drove me.'

'Sometimes you can over identify with a place when you are far from it.'

'Perhaps that is so,' she agreed.

'But you are here,' he said, 'and the critical thing to keep in mind is that you don't drown by falling in the water, you drown by staying there.'

He arose from his chair as if agitated by something, and walked across to the walnut bookcase that covered most of the gable wall. Searching by hand and eye, he finally came across what he was looking for, and withdrew a dog-eared looking paperback.

Turning to her with the sought after book in his hand he said, 'whatever regrets you might have Fuchsia, do not regret leaving your home in Surrey. You didn't run away, you are too intelligent to think for one moment that such a thing is possible. Your grief and anxiety reside in your heart and where you go, they go, but coming here is the first tremulous step to climbing out of the water.'

'I...' he paused wondering if this was the time to share a confidence. 'I know someone, who suffered deeply due to the loss of a child and I hasten to add that the circumstances were very different from yours. This someone did not move away, and consequently not only could she not move on, but neither could anyone around her. Sometimes a physical move is a necessity. Imagine a world full of Miss Havishams.'

She nodded her head, taking from the tenor of his voice that agreement was being called for, although in reality she had barely caught the drift of his speech.

He saw the bemused, confused look on her face, and smiled. 'I'm afraid I have been boring you,' he said, 'stop me when I get carried away.'

'Not at all,' she replied. 'I was just thinking about something, that's all.'

He leant forward in his seat and spoke in a light and confidential tone. 'I have a great fascination with Danish writers and I suspect Father Ryan, the parish priest here, takes that as proof that I am soft in the head, which is probably true, but has nothing to do with my liking for the writers Denmark has produced.'

'I see nothing soft about that Father,' she replied. 'I worked in Copenhagen some years ago and I loved it, especially the people.'

'I have always been fascinated with Scandinavia, especially Denmark,' Salmon told her, 'and I am intrigued by the writers that have hailed from there; they have a unique perspective.'

'I don't know much about Danish writers,' she replied slowly, 'apart from Hans Christian Andersen, who everyone knows. He wasn't from Copenhagen; he came from a port town some distance away from the capital.'

'That is absolutely right,' Salmon said delighted to have engaged her, 'he came from a place called Odense and although he was a natural born storyteller, there wasn't a drop of Irish blood in him as far as anyone knows,' he paused to take a sip from his drink before continuing.

'A lot of people dismiss Denmark as just a clean and tidy Scandinavian country, as it is easy to forget their Viking past. They have produced some fine writers apart from Andersen, such as Søren Kierkegaard and Sigrid Undset, and of course Isak Dinesen.'

'I must confess I have never heard of her,' Fuchsia replied quietly. 'I am familiar though with Sigrid Undset; she too had a brush with scandal.'

'Undset was born in Denmark,' Salmon replied, ignoring the insinuation, 'but raised in Norway and, like Isak Dinesen, she was rather unusual in being a Scandinavian who converted to Catholicism. But, it is this fellow who grips my attention right now.' He held up the book he had just retrieved from the bookshelf and revealed a very old and tattered edition of 'The fairy tales of Hans Christian Andersen'. Carefully flicking through the book, he exclaimed when he reached the page he was after, 'ah this is what I am looking for, The Ugly Duckling.'

He held the book up to show her an illustration of a tatty, bedraggled looking bird walking through what appeared to be marshland.

'Do you know that Andersen once claimed that this story was his autobiography? It is, of course, a fairy tale, but like a lot of fairy tales, it is really a story about redemption and recovery.'

'There are lots of ugly ducklings Father,' she replied with an edge of cynicism in her voice, 'ducklings that never become swans, so where, I'd like to know, is their redemption?'

'All redemption, Fuchsia, ultimately rests on hope, which is the backbone of life.'

She turned her head aside and laughed, and he caught a glimpse of how deep her bitterness ran. 'Like I told you before Father, I am with Nietzsche and, as he put it, hope is the worst of all evils because it prolongs the torment of humans.'

'Well I have to disagree,' he replied emphatically, as if he were contesting an economic or political fact that he found preposterous, 'and it is not in my nature to support name calling, however, on this occasion I am with Tolstoy when he said Nietzsche was stupid and abnormal.'

'He was someone who spoke a good deal of sense.' she replied defensively. 'He also said, when one has not had a good father, one must create one; as someone who has spent most of her life trying to do just that, I can only applaud the man's insight.'

Like a tennis player desperate to keep a ball in service, Salmon immediately sprang back. 'Given the amount of time philosophers spend drooling over books and thinking, they are bound to say something of worth at least once in a lifetime,' he said, and looked at her with a sudden smile that soothed her with its warmness.

'But just because a dog can be trained to walk on its hind legs, there is no reason to suppose it can read a map.'

'Not even Wolf?' she asked

'Maybe I'll make an exception for him,' he replied, 'and of course, even I can overcome my pride and admit that, on this occasion Nietzsche, was absolutely right to articulate the need to create a good father if one has the misfortune to be born either without one, or worse still, with a very bad one.'

Barnabas Salmon sought to engage Fuchsia Delaney with numerous disparate subjects every time he met her, and by doing so, he developed a deeper understanding of her as the person she had been before grief had intruded so rudely into her world. He learnt that she had felt compelled to come to Ireland, to West Cork in particular, to assuage an emotional emptiness that had dominated her for most of her life. Worryingly, he also recognised that the despair that engulfed her was not something that could be easily reasoned with or firmly dismissed. She was an example of what he had discussed during his sermon on suicide. Fuchsia Delaney was undermined as a human and drowning in a sea of doubt, in all its many facets. Her baby had died and she had survived, and for that, she would never forgive herself. What sealed this disenchantment was that, even before the fateful night of the accident, she had never possessed peace of mind. With every word she uttered he noted the terrible loneliness at the heart of her life. Now in the aftermath of the worst having happened, the very essence of existence presented itself too clearly and too starkly. She could look back, without any need to soften the blow, and see that she had never possessed either happiness or purpose, and that life up to this crucial point had been lived out of habit rather than desire.

Her position both anguished and troubled Barnabas Salmon. He sensed that she was struggling with an innate fear, tinged with desire, of her children being abandoned just as she herself had once been abandoned. This woman represented the lost sheep for which the church had been established to care, and it was failing in its mission because few shepherds were actively searching for them. The church had become an institution rather than a body, too preoccupied with its rules and regulations. 'I will put my law in their minds and write it in their hearts.' What is written remains, Salmon told himself, but to what purpose if it is not acted upon?

The parable of the Sheep and the Goats was interpreted far too literally, with the consequences being that if someone was not actually starving or naked or housed in a physical prison, there was no onus to be concerned about them.

Salmon believed that Fuchsia Delaney was starving. She was starved of human affection, starved of the knowledge regarding her identity, and having moved her family at a considerable emotional price, she had discovered that, far from alleviating that spiritual hunger, she was still starved. She was held apart by a community far too insular to consider, and so understand, that the needs of the stranger often went beyond a casual greeting.

However would she break through the barrier of the warm nod and wave that most locals reserved for visitors? He had sympathy for her and empathy for a close- knit community where generations had been bound together by fear of the outsider. They were the creation of a history that taught that fear of the stranger who was not merely passing through, was an eminently sensible thing. The Saxons had arrived and, after initially appearing benign, had gone on to create mayhem. It had taken them almost eight hundred years to get the message that they were not wanted.

Yet the people of the area proclaimed themselves a Christian people, but the essential heart of Christianity was being missed. There was no usefulness in a faith that believed in the possibility of moving physical mountains if it was indifferent to touching the spiritual heart of another.

The reaction of the parish priest towards Fuchsia Delaney confirmed Salmon's observation. Father Ryan, without question, had a great affinity with his parishioners, mainly due to knowing most of them since they were children, but this rapport did not stretch to strangers. He noted the blonde woman's visits to the presbytery, but the only enquiry he ever made about her was regarding to her children's eligibility for certain sacraments.

Salmon placed her burden along with the ones that nestled most deeply within his own heart. No matter how weary the journey or how long the road, some burdens just have to be carried.

Chapter Sixteen

On Dover Beach

Donal Ryan had some extraordinary news for Barnabas Salmon. A parish in the extreme west of the county of Cork, which for administrative reasons came under the remit of the neighbouring diocese of Kerry, was to, at long last, get a new parish priest. The last incumbent had died of old age, and rumour had it that the church would close and the parish would amalgamate with another one some distance away. Now, it appeared, those plans were to be shelved, for a priest who had served in a parish in the south east of England was being sent as the replacement. Donal Ryan was taken aback by Salmon's reaction to his news for, initially, as Ryan had filled him in with all the small inconsequential details and tittle tattle regarding the deceased priest and his fondness for drink, Salmon had barely paid attention. However, when he finally got around to mentioning the name of the priest and the parish in England that he was leaving, Barnabas Salmon had slapped the table in delight.

'Good God Donal,' he had said, knocking the marmalade pot over in his excitement. 'I believe that is Brendan O'Sullivan who served with me in South London, many moons ago.'

'So you know him?' Ryan said, stating the obvious.

'Know him? I should say so, he was the most charismatic and devoted priest the diocese of Southwark ever knew, and why he was allowed to go to the back of beyond, well I'll never know.'

'He is on his way now to the beyond of the beyond,' Ryan replied sourly. 'It's just as well Salmon that you know here and now, that he is leaving his parish in England in some disgrace.'

'Brendan, in disgrace,' Salmon replied incredulously, 'never, the man was a loveable scallywag, full of mischief, but a priest with a heart of gold. I would never believe a word against him.'

'Then either your friend was much maligned or your judgement is quite impaired,' Ryan stated somewhat flatly. Salmon looked at him quizzically for a moment, and wondered quietly to himself if the parish priest realised how unpleasantly sanctimonious he sounded.

As soon as breakfast had finished, Barnabas Salmon had sat down and written a letter to his dear friend. The very moment Brendan O'Sullivan had received it, he had phoned Salmon and asked him to get over in double quick time since he couldn't wait to meet his dear friend once again. He would have come to Droumbally, but he wasn't in want of a horse shoe nail so much as a new battery for his car.

Barnabas Salmon had worked with Brendan O'Sullivan many years previously when they had both served at a large South London parish, which at the time had had five priests attached to it. The pair of them had become great friends, as well as trusted colleagues, until the powers-that-be had seen, in their wisdom, to break the parish up. This sent Salmon to a parish nearer central London, and the younger, gregarious O'Sullivan to a small parish that mainly served the needs of elderly parishioners in rural deepest Kent. Now to Salmon's joy, O'Sullivan was coming back to his native Ireland to take up a position as parish priest some forty kilometres away from Droumbally.

Brendan O'Sullivan was a giant big bear of a man originally from Roscommon. He had turned to the priesthood after spending a few years in the Australian outback where he had worked at a large sheep station. Because of this experience, his entire ministry was formed around the image of the Good Shepherd, which he believed summed up the entire role and reason for religious ministry. After his ordination he had gone on to serve in the foreign missions of South America and, perhaps because of this, his theology, which had always been people centred, had grown steadily more liberal. This, combined with his naturally charismatic and viva-cious personality, had earned him many enemies, from within both the ranks of the hierarchy and the old guard in the laity, who have a presence in virtually every Catholic parish. The latter had kept a watchful eye on the popular priest and had been quick to inform their respective bishops whenever he had strayed too far in preaching the spirit rather than the letter of the law.

He was a handsome man, now in his early sixties, and having been a hurling champion in his youth, he was now paying the price with his aching limbs. He was, at heart, a great humanitarian, and although he had enjoyed a comfortable upbringing, his natural affinity was always with the underdog.

The whole of Salmon's expressive face suddenly lit up the moment O'Sullivan opened his door to greet him, and he was delighted to see that his old friend was every bit as impressive as Salmon remembered. O'Sullivan ushered the English priest into his home, shifting boxes with his feet as he made his way to a ramshackle and poorly resourced back kitchen.

'Sit yourself down Barty,' he said, 'take no notice of the place, it is a tip now and it will still be a tip in the years to come.'

'Well you haven't changed you old rascal,' Salmon replied removing a pile of books from the chair that O'Sullivan had pointed to, 'and thank God for that.'

'And what about you?' asked Brendan. 'Are you wowing them over in Droumbally with your theatrics? I'd say they are a tough crowd, especially with that voice of yours.'

'All changed but all same, if you get my drift,' Salmon replied.

'I do, indeed I do.'

Brendan O'Sullivan was as affable, good- natured and breezy as ever, and yet Salmon perceived that under all the humour and banter, his friend felt diminished in some particular way. They spent some time reminiscing about old times and people who had gone before them.

'Do you remember that time when we went to visit that old couple who lived in the high rise flats near Walworth,' Salmon asked, 'and the geese who came hissing along the balcony?'

'I'll never forget it,' O'Sullivan replied rolling his eyes heavenward. 'I never knew until that day that you could do a twenty yard sprint so niftily.'

'I'd reckon you didn't come across many gaggles of geese cooped up in flats in coastal Kent.'

'Too right,' O'Sullivan agreed, with a sudden look of resignation. 'I came across a different type of old bird there, the sort that rarely spoke, yet could kick up World War Three if I so much as suggested changing a Mass time by half an hour.'

'Coastal Kent was never a hotbed of activity,' Salmon commented, 'I wonder how you stuck it.'

'I didn't, that is why I am here,' O'Sullivan replied quietly, 'and I will be honest with you Barnabas, I am finding it difficult to see my way forward. I feel I have been struggling for so long and now I am at the end and have to face that I have accomplished nothing.'

He then relayed to Salmon the nature of the allegation that had been made against him and Salmon listened attentively and silently, appalled at the treatment his friend had received. A false accusation of an affair with a married parishioner had been made against O'Sullivan, and even though it had been conclusively proved to be a malicious charge, the hierarchy and certain parishioners had ditched the premise of 'innocent until proved guilty'. A heavy and painful silence fell upon the two friends as both struggled to comprehend the destruction that can be wrought by words, never mind actions.

'I met a young woman recently,' Salmon remarked, and O'Sullivan looked at him quizzically, wondering uneasily at the relevance of this revelation at this particular moment.

'She is in the grip of despair, Brendan,' Salmon continued, looking over at his friend whose face had regained its impassive expression. 'She has good reason for it, but the more I listened to her, the more I realised that even if the tragedy that befell her hadn't happened, she would still be a lost soul and few would recognise it, least of all herself. A final straw can break the back of a camel, but too often we examine it to the exclusion of all the straws that went before.'

'Tread easy Barnabas,' O'Sullivan replied, wearily. 'I never thought the day would come when I would say that, but you must protect yourself. She will find a way forward, we all do eventually.'

'I question that outcome with regards to this woman,' Salmon replied. 'She is in the thrall of Nietzsche, but if you heard her story you might understand why.'

'Oh I doubt that Barty,' O'Sullivan replied, shaking his head and making an effort to sound more cheerful. 'He might have been a genius of sorts, but he was too flawed to be taken seriously, certainly as a philosopher. He might have passed as a psychologist, but then Delaney's Donkey was pretty good at reading people too.'

Salmon winced slightly at the mention of the name Delaney, but nodded his head in agreement.

'I agree Brendan,' Salmon said, 'but even so Nietzsche had a way with words. I have never had the time of day for him, but he was spot on about not staring into the abyss for fear that it will stare into you. I find the Atlantic coastline magnificent, but the sea, for all its beauty, is not necessarily tranquil.'

'It is a damn sight more tranquil than the Elephant and Castle,' O'Sullivan replied.

'I wouldn't be so sure,' Salmon argued, 'with traffic and lights and people there is vibrancy, you have to be on your wits looking without rather than within. I would like to see some research into whether or not the counties with the longest Atlantic coastlines have a higher suicide rate.'

'I would hazard a guess that they do,' O'Sullivan replied, 'but there are contributory factors other than the sea, such as rural isolation, lack of jobs and opportunity, and fear of marrying a relative, of course.'

'Absolutely,' Salmon agreed, with a smile at the insinuation. 'I would not doubt for one minute that other factors are involved, but I still hold to the idea that the allure of water is not conducive to calm. It is mesmerizing, it encourages reflection and, above all, it is ceaselessly stimulating; unlike traffic, it never takes a rest.'

'You can say that again,' Father Brendan interjected, 'it has hardly stopped tipping down since I arrived here.'

'Well there is that too,' Salmon conceded, 'and Lord knows the weather could drive an angel to drink, but water itself is deadly, it has a tantalizing nature that beckons the unwary.'

'What was the poem? Something about a daughter asking if she can go for a swim, and the mother saying yes darling daughter, hang your clothes on a hickory limb, but don't go near the water.'

'Great advice,' Salmon said with a smile, 'I just wish more people would follow it.'

'You can drown, Barnabas, without ever putting a toe near the water.'

For a moment, an unnatural melancholic silence fell between them, and when Salmon looked into the face of his friend he saw that it had changed yet again. The temporary animation had disappeared, and in its place was weariness and lifelessness.

'I came across an old poem the other day and the moment I read it I felt it was almost prophetic for our time. And it might be coincidental Brendan, but it resonates with much of what you have said to me today.'

'You know full well I have never been one for poetry,' Brendan replied, with the faintest hint of a smile. 'I'm pure philistine.'

'Poetry has never really been my thing either,' Salmon confessed, 'but I came upon "Dover Beach" quite by chance, and in the light of everything it strikes me as almost foreboding. "The Sea of Faith / Was once, too, at the full… / But now I only hear / Its melancholy, long, withdrawing roar". Of course, at the time Arnold was writing, the world was being turned on its head mainly on account of the discovery of the theory of evolution and the threat it posed to Christian doctrine.'

'The world as we know it now is being turned on its head even as we speak,' O'Sullivan replied. 'Come to think of it, I do recall reading some stuff about Arnold once, what was it he said, something about man cannot do without Christianity, but cannot do with it as it is. Just fancy, over a hundred years later, the same thing holds true.'

'Yes, but the truth also remains that the world stripped of religious certainties, as depicted in Dover Beach, has a nightmare quality to it,' Salmon replied. 'We have to cling on even when it seems the branch itself is falling from the tree.'

The two friends spoke late into the evening and the course of their conversation covered everything from times past to the future of the church, and indeed the world itself. It was late when Salmon reluctantly took his leave. He knew that O'Sullivan would present a cheerful and courageous face to the world, but come the hours of darkness, thought and memory would become his dreaded companions. He drove thoughtfully along the mountainous road and stopped the car for a moment as too many concerns conflicted in his mind. Strife was part of human existence and had been since the day of human creation, it would only cease when the world returned to the home for which mankind had been created for. The night sky was dim save for a few dispersed stars, and his thoughts turned to O'Sullivan sitting in the dark literally and metaphorically, and yet in that moment he could only recall the times when the man had seemed larger than life itself. Although it was difficult to grasp, he thought tenderly, it was a very fortunate fact that in times of darkness, while man is at his weakest, God is most powerful.

Chapter Seventeen

God is Surely in the Detail

Barnabas Salmon dedicated much thought to the needs and revelations of his friend and continued to keep in contact with him by phone and letter. Donal Ryan was intrigued by the friendship, and while he was anxious to know more about the scandal that had sent O'Sullivan west, he had the decency and courtesy not to question Salmon outright about it, although he did drop the occasional not-so-subtle hint.

Not a day passed that Salmon did not offer a prayer of intercession on how best he might help Brendan O'Sullivan, and one morning as the rural gentleman set out to post a letter, he did so unaware that his prayer was finally about to be answered. He dropped the letter into the post box and hesitated for a moment, unsure about whom he should visit first, but the dog began tugging at his lead. Salmon found himself practically being taken for a walk by Wolf as the dog headed enthusiastically in direction of the beach. As he walked with the dog along the strand, he saw Fuchsia Delaney walking towards him. It had been a few weeks since she had last called to the presbytery, and he was delighted to see her and happy to note that the feeling was mutual.

They walked in companionable silence until they reached the sea wall whereby Salmon unhitched the dog from his lead, and began to tell Fuchsia Delaney about his gregarious friend who was now the parish priest in a small community, far off the beaten track.

'He will most likely see out his days there,' he told her, 'but the area is not entirely alien to him for although he hails from Roscommon, his mother was from Bantry originally.'

'The church sounds a very harsh institution,' she replied, after a pause. 'A man like him, and you as well Father should be in a city where you would have much more influence, not in a backwater like this, as beautiful as it is.'

'I thank you for the compliment my dear,' he said, 'but while, in the secular world, the church appears to be an institution, it is, in fact, the mystical body of Christ; only with humans at the helm it doesn't always come across like that. You are spot on about Brendan, though, he is a good and holy man, and very sympathetic to the flaws and tribulations of others.'

She made no reply and, for a moment, the two of them stared out to sea. On the distant horizon, a large boat was sailing into invisibility while along the shoreline an assortment of gulls had congregated in noisy clumps.

'Do you remember,' he said, turning to face her, 'me telling you about the Danish writer Isak Dinesen?

Well, she said that the cure for everything is salt water, be it in the form of sweat, tears or the sea. Who can reject the siren call of the shore?'

'You and your Danish writers,' she replied with a small smile, and Salmon was encouraged by the sheer casualness of her reply.

'Yes' he replied, almost vaguely as if deep in thought about something else. 'The Danish writers and thinkers of the past were acutely aware of being surrounded by water. That might sound obvious but they offered the sea a measure of respect and healthy suspicion, never underestimating its capacity for good or ill. It is why they are such balanced people. Søren Kierkegaard, for example, saw very clearly that faith and doubt go hand in hand. Some things are naturally made to go together like scent and roses, or sheep and a shepherd, or....'

'But for those who have no faith, there can only be doubt,' she interrupted.

'Ah,' Salmon pounced like a cat on a mouse, 'that's not quite true, faith brought doubt into the world, but doubt is ultimately conquered by faith. That is not to say that faith can't, in turn, be nourished by periods of doubt.'

She made no response, and he turned to look at her, suddenly anxious that he may have appeared too dogmatic and so have frightened her away before he could tell her about an idea that he was working up the courage to share.

'Will we take a coffee?' he asked and she nodded her head in agreement. He led the way to Tom Murphy's Boxing Hare bar. It was mid- morning and the long wooden floored café bar had only a few customers. A small group of American tourists were sitting at a table near the bar area, and Tom Murphy was giving them a condensed talk on the flora and fauna of the area. He broke off mid-flow and acknowledged the priest and his companion.

'Talking of migrant species,' he said to the Americans, 'here is one right before your eyes, a rare old breed seldom seen in Ireland but a mark of how far we have come; a priest who has come all the way from England to preach to the rebels.'

His voice was jovial even though his sentiment was slightly barbed, but Salmon ignored that and chose to play along with Murphy, who he suspected was performing for the benefit of the Americans. He did wonder, though, if Tom Murphy realised that, in the eyes of intelligent people, his performance actually belied how far Ireland had really travelled.

The Americans were courteous and the actor in Barnabas urged him not to disappoint, so he enunciated his words more clearly than ever, and put in a good sprinkling of words like 'actually' and 'chap' as he reiterated the landlord's claim that this was, indeed, an enchanting area.

He ordered two coffees, and Fuchsia followed him to a table near the window that offered a panoramic view of the estuary. He was perfectly aware that, by being in the company of an attractive blonde haired woman, he was setting himself up to be the subject of enough conversations to carry Tom through the entire winter, but it failed to concern him.

A young Polish girl brought them their coffee, and while Salmon could hardly contain himself from gulping his down, Fuchsia Delaney hardly touched hers. He asked her if she would prefer something else instead, but she declined with just the barest trace of a smile. From that smile, he detected a personality that always sought to please and he felt a familiar stab of pity and misery stir in his own heart. For the first time, she initiated the conversation.

'Do you ever despair,' she said, 'at the inability of some people to speak words that are not laden with hidden meaning?'

'Worse still,' he replied confidentially in a low voice, 'is the half compliment laced with envy or as some would have it "the bad tongue". Silence is no great indicator either because if a heart is seething with hate, it just means someone is jabbering away internally.'

Her comment caused him to reflect, once again, on her protective nature. As a young man, it had always intrigued and astonished him how people who had been hurt often managed to remain uncontaminated by their experiences. Now, as an older man, he merely admired it.

'Remember Fuchsia,' he said gently, 'many people do not have the faintest idea about what their words actually mean, or even why they are saying them, sometimes. People allowed themselves to be bamboozled into calling for a murderer to be set free and so paved the way for the King of Peace to be slain. We are all guilty of it from time to time.'

She remained silent and he too kept his counsel. The pair sat in companionable silence that was interrupted occasionally by sporadic bursts of enthusiasm by one or other of the Americans, whom Tom Murphy was continuing to charm.

Eventually the Americans took their leave with much hullabaloo and urgings from Tom to come back again, and to take it easy on the road, for there were blighters about who would have them in the hedge in a twinkling of an eye. Once the bar was empty, Tom Murphy made his way to where Salmon and Fuchsia sat.

'God, but they would talk the hind legs off a donkey,' he informed them in a friendly and genial way. Salmon smiled at him, recognising the businessman in action, and Tom began wiping a nearby table, even though it had not been used.

'It's grand weather for the time of year,' he said, looking enquiringly at the conspicuous couple, 'you are wise to get out and about and make the most of it.'

It was obvious from the flirtatious look in his eye that he was fishing for information about Salmon's companion. The priest knew that Fuchsia was not in the form for any interrogation, no matter how friendly or well intentioned. He leaned forward and asked her the time, effectively cutting Tom out of the conversation.

Like the red fox, to whom strategy is all, Tom took the hint, gave up his pretence of cleaning, and made his way back to the bar where he began rearranging bottles and glasses, all the while keeping an eye on the handsome stranger accompanying the priest. Salmon, well aware of the nature of Tom's interest, quietly asked Fuchsia if she was ready to go and she nodded. Walking towards the bar, he placed a sum of money on the counter and, bidding Tom a cheery farewell, he left without waiting for his change, thereby depriving Tom, who he liked immensely, the opportunity of putting his foot in his mouth in the guise of friendly banter.

They parted company at the school gate, but before saying farewell, Salmon turned to his companion and said. 'There is something I would like to suggest to you Fuchsia.'

While he had stood beside her at the beach looking into the beyond, an idea so overwhelming in its obviousness had struck him straight out of the blue ocean. Both Fuchsia Delaney and Brendan O'Sullivan were immersed in grief; her for the loss of her baby and him for loss of his vocation. Salmon knew that for a priest, despair is nothing short of an admission that his entire life has been a fraud. O'Sullivan was the Shepherd, and she was the lost sheep, they could restore and nurture each other.

Neither the shepherd nor the sheep were keen to engage with Salmon in his great plan. O'Sullivan shook his head in dismay when Salmon suggested that no one was in a better place to offer hope, than one who feared losing it.

'Brendan, you told me years ago that the mission of a priest is to be where the wound is, and this woman is wounded; she is lost, but I have every faith that you can find her. It is what you have always done; you need proof that you can do it again.'

The big man was still smarting from his own wounds and fearful of letting the woman down, but Salmon remained implacable in his belief that O'Sullivan could show her the way forward. Eventually he agreed to at least meet with her, if only to appease Salmon.

Fuchsia Delaney, who had never been observant in the practise of her faith, was even more wary. Salmon had confounded all her beliefs in what priests were really like, but even so, the thought of meeting yet another one was almost too hard to take. In the end rather like the shepherd, she only agreed to meet with O'Sullivan in order to please Salmon.

'I think this God you believe in,' she said to Salmon, as they drove along the mountainous road towards the parish where O'Sullivan lived, 'is very careless about the crosses he hands out.'

'I read somewhere once that it was Sigrid Undset's belief that many a man is given what is intended for another, but no man is given another's fate. I can't tell you how much those words used to reassure me, back in the day when I was an aspiring actor.' He paused a moment to concentrate more carefully on the road, for driving was something that didn't come naturally to him.

'Great works of literature rarely make for happy reading, even if some happen to end happily,' she replied. 'The unhappy ones just introduce more misery and the happy ones mainly represent a world you know can never exist.'

'That is true to an extent,' he agreed, 'but to tell you the truth, my interest is seldom in the tale but in the story behind the teller. Tolstoy, Dickens, Hugo, Undset and indeed Andersen all travelled long and complicated roads, most of them profoundly unhappy ones. It is a cliché Fuchsia, but life really is a journey. The pity, though, is that the very people who bandy that cliché around rarely focus on the destination, which for a Christian, of course, is ultimately heaven. Some grasp it very early on in life while for others it is a last minute realisation.'

'Sometimes,' she said turning her face to the window, 'I feel as if religion is obsessed with death. Perhaps Beckett had it right, we are born into the grave and life is all about coming to terms with that unsavoury fact.'

'Yes,' he replied, 'I can see that many people must feel like that, but then birth and death are the two things every living thing has in common. The secular world is also obsessed with death, you only have to look at the news or entertainment, its effect in the main is depressing because it seldom tackles what lies beyond.'

'Death defines us,' she said turning to look at him almost in the hope that he might contradict her. 'In the way water defines land, death defines life. We all know how it is going to end but the journey is not the same for everyone.'

He stopped the car as they reached the highest point on the steep road, and for a moment in silence the pair looked at the panoramic view ahead of them, which took in the sweeping valley and the glistening ocean in the mid distance.

'Strange as it may seem, you have reminded me of something I was thinking about only recently,' he told her. She remained silent as if entranced by the view.

'It is no secret that I love Christmas,' he said, and upon hearing this she gave him a startled glance since that great feast was still some distance away.

'But,' he continued, 'I rather think sometimes that as a feast it is a wasted opportunity, because the greatest feast of all from mankind's point of view is surely the Ascension. That is the feast about which the church should have made the greatest hullabaloo.'

'But the church has always been practical,' she replied. 'Christmas dominates because it takes place in bleak winter.'

'True,' he agreed, 'and many think that since Christianity hijacked the pagan festival, the secular one can hijack the Christian one. If, however, the Ascension had been the feast on which the church had focused, it would be an entirely Christian affair. All hearts and minds would be fixed on where we all, ultimately, want to aim. What a celebration it would be.'

'Celebrating our inevitable demise,' she replied, with the faintest hint of a bemused smile, 'somehow I don't think that would have caught on.'

'As a last resort,' he said cheerfully, 'I must return to Hugo, "it is nothing to die. It is frightful not to have lived." If only more people considered that prospect, the world would be a happier place.'

She remained silent appearing to be deep in thought, and Salmon looked questioningly, summoning up the courage to say what he believed had to be said.

'You are on a unique journey Fuchsia,' he said, his voice suddenly both serious and quiet. 'One you never wanted to undertake; and the place from which you are starting is dark and dangerous. As the proverbial man said, "if I wanted to go there, I wouldn't want to be starting from here." When we first met on that beach, you asked me "what is truth?" Well the truth is Fuchsia, is that you are where you are; no one envies your position, but the journey cannot be abandoned and neither are there any shortcuts.'

'There is a shortcut, and I have often considered taking it,' she replied.

'The wise are always open to consideration,' he replied, 'but to die by choice is to close yourself off to the possibility that you will rediscover the beauty that is life. The answer to everything is love. Choose life and live in the hope that the lives of your children will be as rich in joy as yours has been in misery.'

For the first time since he met her, he saw in her face the light of hope, and sensed that she, at last, was considering the possibility of there being a road ahead.

'Nothing can be endured or understood without love,' he remarked, switching the engine back on, 'and love shows its face in so many different ways. The tragedy is our scandalously poor ability to interpret it.'

So, once again the wisdom of Salmon prevailed. As the weeks and months passed, he saw a transformation slowly unfold in both O'Sullivan and Fuchsia Delaney as both discovered the ability to trust again, not just in themselves, but in others as well.

Nothing could undo her past, but with trust, she could avert the tragedy of failing to countenance a brighter future. Moreover, she could consider the possibility of happiness. As for Brendan O'Sullivan, he discovered during his discourses with Fuchsia Delaney, that the admission that he only knew that he knew nothing, was a virtue rather than a vice. Henceforth, he would be humbly content to be both the confidant and confider; he could bear his doubts.

Right to the end, Father Ryan's stoicism also prevailed; for he had never once enquired about the visits of the woman or indeed, why they dribbled to a virtual halt.

'I hear that Delaney woman had a son,' he told Salmon one day as he prepared to head for a greyhound meet in the city, 'and from all accounts he was killed in a car accident. She was the driver, apparently. I don't know all the details, but I suppose that accounts for her looking like a bird wandering from her nest most of the time.'

Salmon had merely nodded. Ryan was certainly right about one thing, he didn't know all the details; nobody ever did. There was much more to the story of Fuchsia Delaney, Salmon thought wistfully. He had no idea what it was; only that God was surely in the details.

But, he thought philosophically as he headed into the study, it was ever this way. The keystone was always to be found in the seemingly unimportant details. He thought about the marriage of Eddie Moran and Carolyn O'Shea, and the meticulous planning that would have gone into their grand wedding: the booking of the reception and the choosing of the dress, the suit, the cake and the attire of the bridesmaids. In all the commotion, a small detail of immense magnitude had been neglected. The seemingly insignificant detail of love had been overlooked, and the show was set to come down because of it.

He never ceased in his prayers for all who had sought his help, but he did lament that some memories just cannot be shared.

Chapter Eighteen

Same Mentality, Different Taboos

In the late autumn of 2009, Barnabas Salmon travelled once again to England to see Clarissa. Some friends were holding a party to mark her recovery, and quite naturally, she was very anxious that Barnabas should be there.

When Salmon arrived home again in West Cork, he announced to his parishioners that Clarissa had been given an official 'all clear' by her doctor, and wanted nothing more than to resume her work, which she loved passionately. There was no doubt that Salmon was overjoyed with Clarissa's good news and he thanked the parish for keeping the stranger in their prayers. However, the more observant parishioners noted that aside from this happiness, Barnabas Salmon was more subdued than they had ever seen him before. They were as yet unaware that he was on the threshold of sharing some startling revelations about Clarissa's life in Kent. Of more significance however was the detail he chose not to reveal, and it was this, on this particular visit to

England, it was he who had sought consolation from Clarissa rather than the other way round.

From the very first moment Father Salmon had ever mentioned Clarissa, the woman's name had conjured up an image in the imagination of many parishioners of a rather sedate pampered woman who lived a well-meaning life in the lap of luxury. He had told them all about her musical accomplishments and her ability with languages. This had confirmed, for many, that Clarissa was the spoilt daughter of a rich man who had graduated from spending her father's money to spending that of her wealthy late husband. For some reason the majority had also pictured her as being a natural blonde, even though Salmon had never physically described her.

It was greeted with some surprise when he informed the parish that Clarissa's son Edward, who had been very attentive to his mother during her illness, had actually followed her example and was himself a journalist, currently employed by an American corporation. The parish learnt that, far from being a relic of a bygone age, Clarissa had always lived a staunchly independent existence. She was a journalist and a writer who had written three well-received books, and who regularly contributed to several BBC programmes including "Woman's Hour" and various features on the world service. Her specialty was not, as the parish might have anticipated, something along the lines of country diaries, but the rather weighty subject of anthropology.

It was soon to become very clear why Father Salmon thought it relevant to tell the parish about Clarissa's occupation. But, what was more shocking by far was her relationship with the subject matter that was to rock not just the parish of Droumbally, but indeed every parish throughout the land.

The Murphy Report into abuse by the clergy of the Roman Catholic Church in Ireland was now ready for publication. It was not the first account of historic depravity, but the contents of this particular report shocked the nation to its core. The shock and horror was not restricted to the horrific details of the actual abuse, but also to the scandalous revelation that there had been observant and uncaring onlookers. The details of their role had surpassed all that had been previously known.

Father Donal Ryan was shell-shocked by the contents. He told Salmon of a priest who had served in the locality who had been jailed some ten years previously for sickening assaults on both boys and girls. 'The man was sick,' he said, by way of explanation, 'everyone who came into contact with him knew he was odd; as it turned out his oddness was severely underrated.'

At first Salmon said nothing. He did not doubt for one minute the sincerity of Ryan's shock and disgust, what he did question though, was his rush to diagnose the man as sick. Where, he wondered, would the likes of Ryan draw the line between sick and debauched? He had an uncomfortable feeling that Ryan might be seeking refuge behind the banner of illness because the other alternative was too distressing to contemplate.

'To quote Tolstoy,' he remarked quietly as much to himself as to Ryan, '"Not according to our desert but according to thy mercy." Let's hope and pray that will be the outcome for all of us.'

'Well I'll say one thing for you Salmon,' Ryan spoke tersely, 'you can always be depended upon to trot out a quote, but for most of the authors who appear to inspire you, I personally would not spare a tinkers curse.'

'Likewise Donal, I always depend on your charity, but I assure you many of the authors you so casually dismiss could be relied upon to shine a light of reality on the tragedy that is Murphy.'

'Tragedy is a good word,' Ryan conceded, 'and no effort must be spared in letting people know that we understand the devastation, but we have to rightly point out the historical nature of Murphy.'

'I really fear you just might be trying to wind me up,' Salmon replied, with an air of disbelief. He stood up and walked briskly towards the window where he stopped and swung round to glare at Ryan from the twin vantage points of light and height.

'This is not a time for history Donal,' he said, his voice flecked with annoyance, 'this is not historical nonsense, this is an evil that each generation makes new.'

Ryan flinched and straightened his back against his chair, each hand tightly gripping the arm of the tapestry armchair. He was visibly shocked by Salmon's outburst and yet he cleaved to his cause.

'Oh for God's sake Salmon, don't let's start on recriminations, what is past is past. Do you think it will serve any purpose to invite parishioners to dwell on wrongdoing, to irresponsibly dispatch with any notion of leading and join in a chorus of media led denunciation? Have you learnt nothing since you've been in Ireland?'

'Since I've been in Ireland,' Salmon replied incredulously. 'Do you think this is about geography rather than the human condition? Don't even get me started on Ireland Donal; your nose is pressed too close to the window pane, you have no perspective.'

'And I suppose your gadding back and forth to Kent allows you an aerial view,' the priest replied sarcastically, 'you may have a view Salmon, but I have the gut instinct.'

'As a matter of fact,' Salmon replied a little obscurely, 'you rather have it the wrong way round. With Murphy we are getting a glimpse of human nature at its weakest and most corrupt, but believe me Donal, the subject is more complex. Yes, the clergy is under the spotlight, but as the stone gets lifted higher and higher, we are going to see the full glory, including the industrial schools and the Magdalene laundries. In fact if the media are really up for it, we will get a vision into a culture that was, and in some respects still is, rotten from the top down.'

He paused for a moment as if sickened by the words he had uttered. He continued in a strained and emotional voice. 'The rot extends way beyond the church, but the clergy will carry the cross for their own sins and the sins of others, and rightly so.'

'Ha,' Ryan grunted contemptuously, 'there you have it; you think you can lump it all together: clerical abuse, industrial schools and the Magdalene. You are being clumsy Barnabas. You might not understand the difference between all these things, but the people of this parish do.'

'Then I stand ready to be shot down,' Salmon replied quietly, 'but the essence, when all is boiled down to pure concentrate, is that the laundries, the schools and the clerical abuse, even the almighty recession that is going to choke the life out of this country, they all come down to the crass status of the individual. When a society allows that to happen it is as far removed from Christianity as it is possible to be; a Catholic country yes, but a Christian one, never.'

Donal Ryan was discomfited by the assertions of his fellow priest, although in truth he held with much that the man was saying, his hide bound conservative nature, which he liked to believe was nothing more than a desire to uphold tradition, prevented him from acknowledging the possibility of truth. Instead, he fell back on that most Catholic of defences.

'Well I don't know at all Barnabas,' he said with an air of perplexity, 'but the devil has hitched a free ride and he is out to humiliate and subdue the church, it is all very, very worrying.'

This was Ryan's attempt at closing a conversation that he found both distasteful and confusing because it called into question too many preconceived notions. His lack of desire to rise to the challenge only succeeded in making him feel uncomfortably guilty. However, the attempt did not work. Barnabas Salmon turned from the window and walked purposely towards the bookcase where he began rifling amongst the various volumes at a furious rate. When he eventually found what he was looking for, he pulled the book deftly from its resting place and began thumbing through it intently. Looking across at the seated parish priest, he spoke a little breathlessly.

'Sometimes Donal the clergy are like stopped clocks, no matter what year, what decade what century even, the same old excuses get churned out. Look at this here, have you ever read it?'

Donal Ryan lifted tired, but contemptuous looking eyes up so that he could see the book Salmon was holding, and shook his head.

'The Nun of Kenmare,' he read aloud with a smile. 'No, I have never read it Barnabas, and I doubt I ever will; from all accounts she was something of a trout and a turncoat.'

'Well,' replied Salmon with an equally contemptuous look, 'from all accounts she was well used to name calling, but whether she was a trout or not is another story. What she was, without question, was both astute and prophetic. I'll not bring the subject up with you again, Donal, because it is obvious we are not going to see eye to eye, but at least listen with an open mind to the words she wrote way back in 1889, and apply them to the bigger picture. Ask yourself if things just might have been different, if this woman, and others like her, had been listened to and respected.'

He began reading aloud to the parish priest who, throughout, kept his face resolutely devoid of any emotion.

'*Roman* Catholic ecclesiastics have impressed the people with the very convenient idea that they are not to be blamed, no matter what wrong they may do; so the "devil" is made the convenient scapegoat. The claim of priests to be thus excused is a serious danger to the Roman Catholic Church. Facts cannot be hidden as they were in earlier ages. People know that certain evils exist, and though they may be silent for a time, the existence of these evils is not forgotten. An open, honest admission of the evils in the church would go far to lessen them. It would at least save the church the awful crime of even appearing to approve evil by not condemning it.'

'It's a viewpoint,' Donal Ryan said indifferently, 'nothing more.'

It was the first serious disagreement the two priests had ever shared, and for some days following it, an atmosphere of dissent settled upon the presbytery. Both listened to the wall-to-wall coverage as witness after witness on the radio and television gave shocking accounts of abuse amid a fervid atmosphere of bitterness and anger. Both men tried to reconcile their own thoughts and feelings with those expressed by their parishioners and the wider community.

Madge Healy had been photocopying the parish newsletter in the small office opposite the sitting room where the two priests had argued. She had heard the raised voices, and had caught the tense atmosphere and the occasional word.

'I think Father Salmon is very insensitive,' she confided to Mary Kelly, who taught at the village National school. 'I think he should respect Father Ryan more than he does on this abuse business.'

'If by respect, Madge,' the schoolteacher had replied disdainfully, 'you mean keep a lid on it all, then I have to tell you this, that Salmon has my respect. This is a tidal wave and frankly, the likes of Ryan – good and well-meaning as he is – who think that pathetic little sandbags of apology are going to work, have had their day.'

Although she was unaware of it at the time, the previously conservative teacher had concisely and succinctly put into words the thoughts and feelings of the vast majority of the community.

It may have been coincidence, but two parents withdrew their children from the altar-serving rota. More than a few others suddenly decided that going to Mass on a Sunday could happily be avoided.

The report continued to be discussed in the shops and bars in the village, and indeed throughout the length and breadth of Ireland. Some fought for the status quo by quoting the "few rotten apples" mantra. Some were cagey in their denunciation, since they still had respect for their own parish priest, but were now highly suspicious of ones they did not know. As for others, hate and fury were the order of the day. It was not a case of innocent until proven guilty, quite the reverse in fact.

Salmon's observation proved to be accurate. The urge to seek distance by resorting to history proved irresistible. Suddenly, people who could hardly remember the previous day's weather were swiftly able to recall every slight they had received at the hands of the clergy. Many were anxious to recall verbal and physical assaults suffered by themselves, but more frequently by their peers, yet few thought to challenge the silence that had once surrounded it all. Even the role of the clergy in the war of independence was reviewed as if it had all occurred recently, and some even recalled the treatment of Parnell as if they had personally been present when it had all happened. The further they looked back into history the further they subtly removed themselves and their own family and society from involvement.

As the priest who celebrated the Saturday vigil Mass, it fell on Salmon to test the water, so to speak, albeit to a smaller than usual congregation.

If he was surprised by them, they were shocked by him. The jaunty, confident thespian they had come to know now appeared somehow smaller and meeker in demeanour, and thoroughly overburdened.

'The gospel,' he said beginning his sermon in a more subdued tone, 'always speaks for itself. Tonight I need to speak to you in the face of an appalling reality, and I am struggling to find the words.'

He paused, and for one electrifying moment, a single thought occupied the minds of many of the people seated in front of him. Was it possible that Father Salmon was going to renounce his priesthood? In the light of recent revelations, anything now seemed possible, and the man did look thoroughly and completely dejected. Seconds passed and eventually he raised his head.

'There are many things I'd like to tell you,' he said slowly, 'but some memories cannot be shared until the time is right, and that moment is not yet here.

'The writer, Victor Hugo, said that every bad institution in the world ends by suicide, and I fear that adage might well be applied to the church; the institutional church, not the mystical body of Christ.

'As a priest, at this very moment I feel humbled, distant and overwhelmingly insignificant standing here in front of you. I thank you for attending Mass in this church tonight because, in all truth, I cannot say that if I were in your place that I too would have made the call.

'Humans are capable of many ills but crimes against the innocent always have the most impact. We are reared on stories concerning wolves destroying the sheepfold, and it is beyond the bounds to learn that shepherds can do the work of wolves. I have found myself thinking deeply about what shapes us as a society, and how society shapes us as individuals.

'My thoughts drove me into this church last night, or should I say during the early hours of this morning. While my mind was crowded with a plethora of difficult thoughts, my eyes caught sight of the old tapestry that hangs in the porch, the one bearing the images of Saints Patrick and Brigid. Somebody long ago, perhaps a parish priest, took the decision to put the two national saints as the backdrop to the church entrance. I looked at them as if I had never seen them before, and I found myself asking if the story today might have been different, if St Brigid had been hailed as the foremost national saint. After all, unlike Patrick, she was actually born and raised here. What if she had been Ireland's foremost national saint, would that in any way have abated the patriarchal dominance that prevails in this society and indeed the priesthood itself? What we have to grasp is that what happened was not merely human nature at its worse, but it was human structures that allowed it to flourish.

'Something is very wrong when it takes a report by a judge to fire the starting gun for a society to begin questioning itself, because we are talking about many deeply scarred people. These were not isolated crimes; aside from the victims, others knew it was happening. As I mentioned briefly, quite recently, Clarissa's area of specialty is anthropology. She studied it at Cambridge. A few years ago, her work brought her to Ireland, and I think it is tragic that she never visited this island as a tourist prior to being given an assignment that introduced her to the terrible world of the Magdalene laundries and all their horrific off shoots.

'I might add that a great many writers, journalist, medics and clergy have long suspected that such a report would one day break through the barrier of denial.

'Through the ages, you as a people have been called by the church to atone for your sins and transgressions. Your literature is full of stories and accounts of less than charitable priests. As a priest of that same church, I beg mercy and forgiveness from you. I take some comfort from the fact that Christ handpicked twelve apostles, and far from being icons of perfection, they deceived, denied and betrayed him. Human nature was the same then as it is now. It is no longer difficult to believe that it was the hierarchy at the time of Christ, the so- called pillars of the community who called for a murderer to be set free, and so paved the way for the suffering servant to meet his end.

'I get some inspiration from Peter, who failed, and yet did not despair like Judas did. By surrendering to hope, Peter turned the very tide upon which he had once walked.

'All of us are guilty of the good we do not do. Many priests and bishops must now examine their consciences before they dare to face God.

'I do, however, get an uneasy feeling that the Murphy report is being presented as a summary, a summing up of things long past with a footnote warning us to be vigilant; vigilant about what exactly? People very blithely talk about history repeating itself; but more often than not, they stop short of quoting Marx in full. What Marx actually said was that history repeats itself first as tragedy, second as farce, and it will be farcical in the extreme, if those who seek to set a new agenda prove to be every bit as tyrannical as those who set the old one.

'I am so very afraid that we will only read Murphy as a tale from the past, and not realise that, perhaps, it also gives us a glimpse into the future as well. We have moved on from the era when a priest or a teacher could lash out at a child for eating meat on a Friday or box their ears upon discovering that they had missed Mass or confession. Even in the era of such occurrences, few people, if they had examined their consciences, could sincerely have believed that Christ would have approved of their actions. We have moved on, thank God, but, now and then, stop and ask, what are the new rules and regulations against which an individual must not transgress? You might inquire as to the relevance of this observation. In a clumsy way I am trying to say that abuse of power stalked the old order, but do not think the new order that will arise from a post-Christian era will necessarily be benign. The mentality will be the same; just the taboos will be different.

'I once spoke to a friend, who was on the brink of despair, quite fleetingly about a poem called Dover Beach, and little did I know how relevant that poem was to become to me. You see, it deals with the spectre of God's existence being cast into doubt, mainly because of new revelations. The poet was trying to make sense of Christianity in the light of newly discovered scientific theories, particularly those concerning evolution. A modern day poet might try to write a new Dover Beach in the light of the Murphy report. Something else in that poem struck me last night as being very relevant to where we are today. In Dover Beach, the poet alludes to an ancient battle that took place at night during the Athenian invasion of Sicily. The soldiers were tired and it was dark, and nothing was clear. In the confusion, they ended up, more often than not, killing members of their own army. We too must be careful, for in the dark and confusion in which we find ourselves; we might be too shocked and stressed to see a way forward or be capable of distinguishing between friend and foe.

'The poem, I am glad to tell you, is not irresistibly pessimistic. The one light in it, are the lovers on the beach who realise that the only thing they can hold on to is love itself.

'Well, we are the lovers waiting on the metaphorical beach. We live in the midst of hope, knowing from our own life experiences that change invariably happens, and how could anyone, at this moment, not long for change; a change of heart but not a knee-jerk reaction.

'Change will, I fear, prove very hard to implement, because it will have to go beyond the confines of the church.

'I have no doubt that a new world order is coming, for much of the old one was bad; rotten to the core. Still I advise you, keep vigilant, for history will repeat itself; but the next wolf will be wearing different clothing.'

For some time after this sermon, a melancholic air hung over Salmon. In the eyes of many, he never fully regained his former sprightliness. It was of course November, the month of the holy souls, which perhaps added to the sense of bleakness and gravity. Those who had attended the vigil Mass carried the details of Salmon's sermon back to the wider community, like rooks carrying restoration back to their nests. By his testimony and acknowledgement concerning the horrors of Murphy's revelations, Barnabas Salmon touched the hearts and minds of all who had witnessed his courage and humility. When Ger O'Reilly, the staunchest critic of Barnabas Salmon, attempted to incriminate the English priest with the brush of scandal one night in Whites bar, the reaction of his audience shocked him. They turned on him with such ferocity and disgust that even O'Reilly had to question his stance. Ever faithful to his contrary nature, Ger felt a sudden inclination to revisit the church, just as others were deciding to leave it.

In his unique way, the grittiness of Barnabas Salmon's sermon polished the gem of faith that remained buried deep within the traumatised faithful. When parishioners retold the story of how the rural gentleman had responded to the scandal, it went some way to rolling back the obstacle the church presented on the path to belief. Many who heard felt a personal desire to rise once again to the new challenge presented by their faith.

Chapter Nineteen

Quality and Quantity

The well-being of Brendan O'Sullivan and the plight of the grief stricken Fuchsia Delaney, along with the fallout from the Murphy report, occupied a great deal of Barnabas Salmon's time and thinking, but he did not neglect those who had come to rely on him. He continued to nurture and to lend a listening ear to a great number of people who sought his help and opinion. Throughout this entire difficult period, he maintained his visits to old Sam Dunne, to the O'Haras who had given him Wolf, and to Bridie Clancy, amongst many others. Eddie Moran, the troubled husband, always looked somewhat bashful whenever he came across the priest, but Salmon treated him as if he had never confessed to anything more substantial than preferring Monday to Tuesday.

Over two years had passed since the arrival of the Saxon priest, who was now referred to, almost without exception, as the Rural Gentleman. Some still found mileage in teasing him about his accent, which remained as crisp and clear as ever, and the intrigue surrounding his visits to England never diminished.

'I'd say it has to be a blonde,' Tom Murphy remarked humorously to some of his regulars at the Boxing Hare. Tom had never quite forgotten seeing the priest in the company of the attractive woman, or forgiven him for not introducing her to him. Since then, Tom had often observed Fuchsia Delaney walking the beach, but the fragile air about her invited no intrusion into her world, so wisely he kept his counsel.

'Well it isn't a sick sister,' John O'Regan, a bad tempered, stocky little man interjected. 'I wouldn't visit mine even if she was on her last legs, never mind cross the sea for the honour.'

This declaration was not greeted with a stunned silence since everyone knew how much O'Regan despised his sister for making a success out of the boom, when all he had achieved was a mountain of debt. There wasn't a tradesman or wholesaler in the area to whom O'Regan didn't owe money, and yet he still drove a decent looking car, lived in a grand house, and all the while managed to maintain a bitter and malevolent demeanour.

Aside from the jokes and innuendo, the community held a profound respect for Salmon. He had spoken about the possibility of an economic collapse long before it was considered decent to do so. He also had the courage of his convictions in speaking openly and sympathetically about suicide, which everyone knew he believed shared common ground with both the threat and reality of a dwindling economy. He was a true shepherd who not only stood with his sheep, but who was constantly on the lookout for imminent dangers to them; be they physical threats to security or spiritual ones whose roots lay deep in unhappy memories.

He was a pastor who urged his flock to believe the best about themselves and each other. What a happy coincidence, then that the very night Ger O'Reilly chose to see what all the commotion concerning Salmon was about, happened to be when the rural gentleman was informing the congregation about the attributes of the parents of General Michael Collins, who, amongst other things, had both been fluent in Greek and Latin.

'I make no pitch for politics,' he told them, 'but Collins grew up in a rural background in a far corner of Ireland and yet held his own with Churchill and the might of the British establishment. It was the vision of his parents that secured him this equality, for they kept a home that was full of the works of Shakespeare and Thomas Hardy, and so he grew to an understanding of the English mind. Take something from their example; ask yourselves if the vision of your children is being restricted by exposure to soap operas and the like. How are they being prepared to understand a wider world? Does anyone think such shows, along with reality television are ever created with the long view in mind? On the other hand, if you do keep a library of the great writers, Irish, British, Russian or whatever, is it purely ornamental? Or is it being used for the purpose for which it was designed?

'In a nutshell, the parents of Collins handed him the DNA of the British and as a consequence, he was able to lead. Now, I can almost hear some of you saying, "well of course it was easier back in the days when there was no television," but take it from me, the past had its own distractions.'

Salmon's visits to Clarissa diminuished to a few scattered ones here and there, but even so, each time he left Ireland he saw it through fresh eyes upon his return. He saw the confidence of the country slipping and he recognised the spectre of denial on the face of many parishioners. More people than ever came to him seeking solace, recognising in the outsider the capacity to be even-handed.

He listened as men told him about debts they were no longer able to pay, and he heard the fears of women who were unable to convince their husband that worries about money should not trump all other concerns. He developed a growing belief that fears of debt were wiping away the capacity for many people to understand true grief.

It also saddened him to see the rise of a divisive mentality, with people who had taken no risk during the boom years pitched against those who had. Father Ryan also had views on this growing scenario.

'It is tough, Barnabas, for people who cannot pay their mortgages,' he agreed, 'but the reality is that these people made a contract and it is hardly fair to expect the prudent, who often live quite frugally, to maintain those who don't.'

'With the greatest respect Donal,' Salmon replied, 'you are dividing people into two extreme camps, those who blew it big time with cars and crazy holidays, and those who accounted for the spending of every penny. There are great swathes in between.'

'I don't doubt that for a minute,' Ryan had replied, 'but I still say it is pushing it to expect the prudent to support the imprudent, the ant to support the grasshopper.'

'Do you think it is possible Donal, that coming from a large farm background, you are being a tad less sympathetic to those who have no such heritage on which to fall back?'

'Well, if that is the case, given your heritage, you must be truly well adrift.'

Salmon did not pursue the subject, for he saw the tip of Ryan's inferiority complex beginning to make an appearance. He could not deny that the local priest had the ear of the farming community, most especially the upper echelons. He knew about their requirements, what they wanted the EU to deliver and the precise weather they required, but he was oblivious to those who made their living from other forms of enterprise. This group sought solace from Salmon.

From the moment he had set foot in the picturesque, rural parish, Barnabas Salmon had recognised it as a microcosm of a society that was undergoing a deep and swift transformation. He had arrived when the economy was at its peak, and although, prior to his arrival, he had known from the media and Irish friends and acquaintances that the republic was booming, it had still come as something of a shock to witness the full scale of the boom.

There had been a time when the contrast between Irish and English attitudes to money had been a source of amusement to him. The aspect that defined the English, he thought, was their great love of getting a bargain. When an Englishman closed a deal securing a car or a holiday at a cheaper rate than a friend or colleague, far from being abashed, it was considered something to brag about. As a priest, he knew all about the imperative of avoiding occasions of sin, but going to the supermarket back in metropolitan Kent had often provided an opportunity for a slice of fun that he wouldn't have avoided for the world. He found the sight of comfortably off people making a mad dash in pursuit of "reduced to clear" items extremely amusing. It was invariably accompanied by a kerfuffle of tension and drama over who got to take home the reduced sausages. It reminded him of the feeding frenzy that occurs when ducks are being fed at a pond. As theatre, it rivalled anything playing in the West End.

Upon his arrival in Ireland in 2007, the first thing he had noticed was the complete reversal in attitude towards money. People in Ireland simply loved spending money, and many had no hesitation in admitting when they had paid over the going rate for something they wanted. A conversation with Anne O'Donovan, a parent governor at the local school, had illustrated this most succinctly. Just a few weeks after Salmon had first arrived, O'Donovan had attended a wedding in Rome and her teenage son had initially declined to accompany her. However, at the very last moment he had changed his mind and as a result, Anne had to pay triple the price she had paid for her own ticket. 'Can you imagine that?'

she had asked the small group assembled around her, 'just fancy, I could have gone to New York two times for the price of it.' Salmon had caught the faintest whisper of a proud boast in her voice. He had immediately reflected that if such a thing happened in Kent, the son in question would have either stayed at home or he would have gone to Rome in the sure knowledge that he would still be listening to recriminations about it come the happy couple's silver wedding anniversary.

Over dinner later that night, he had raised the subject with Father Ryan.

'Many habits and customs that are commonplace in Ireland today,' Ryan had replied informatively, 'have their roots in the days of the famine. An example is the custom of urging hospitality on a visitor, and refusing to take no for an answer, even after several refusals. A person would not accept hospitality because they knew, in reality, that their host had nothing to offer, yet the host, for sake of his or her own pride had to insist. It was a game, both players knew that and that the roles would be reversed one day.'

'All very different to Kent,' Salmon told Ryan, 'over there hospitality is offered on a carousel basis; if you don't take something offered once, you wave it goodbye.'

As the impact of the economic meltdown began to make its presence felt on a daily basis, it soon became clear to Salmon that, just as not everyone had equally shared in the boom, so not everyone was equally sharing in the suffering. Parishioners from the old, established, moneyed and landed families had not had any need of the Tiger. Others, through the astute and timely sale of assets, made themselves more comfortable. They realised they would one day re-purchase, at a fraction of the price, the very property they had sold. Father Ryan stood with them, and although he expressed sympathy to those severely challenged by the twin evils of debt and unemployment, he proved unequivocally that a personal prison is a very hard place to escape from.

This did not diminish Salmon's respect for the parish priest. He understood that the man was in the grip of the results of both his nurture and his nature. He also suspected that Ryan was partly motivated by a fear of which he wasn't even fully aware, since he fully subscribed to the school of thought that refusal to acknowledge despair was rewarded by a measure of protection from it.

In essence, however, Salmon was someone who spoke about the past while preferring the hope offered by the future, whereas Ryan was simply someone who felt more comfortable in the security of the past and rarely entertained thoughts concerning the future.

As the recession bit ever deeper, more local businesses failed, and more young people left the area. A crescendo was reached when a politician directly contradicted an assertion made by a journalist, only for it to be revealed just hours later that, contrary to what the politician had so vigorously denied, the IMF were already in Ireland.

As the days and weeks flew past, the evidence accumulated and even Father Donal Ryan had to adapt his views and agree that, while some sections of the population were immune to the downturn, a significant sector were immersed and overburdened with misery.

He even took to quoting Yeats, repeatedly telling Salmon that Romantic Ireland was dead and gone. To his surprise, the literary Salmon did not respond to his newly found fondness for poetry. In truth, Salmon thought that Ryan was showing up very late to the party, for in his opinion, Romantic Ireland was long dead and gone. It wasn't the appearance and subsequent disappearance of the so-called Tiger that was at fault either. He found the fallout from the economic crash a difficult subject to discuss with Ryan, and the only person to whom he could confide his concerns was his old friend Brendan O'Sullivan, who was, at last, beginning to find his equilibrium.

From what Salmon could determine, Romantic Ireland had long ago been hijacked and clinically euthanized by the Irish state. He saw modern Ireland through the eyes of the Irish emigrants he had known in England, and was more convinced than ever, that the population were being brainwashed into thinking that government control was a manifestation of civilization. Blind patriotism, he believed led to a denial of rights and was a footstep along the path to authoritarianism.

He didn't doubt for one moment that many of the Irish he had known in England looked back on their native land with rose coloured glasses. Some were just too hurt or too damaged to acknowledge the truth about why they had left. They were wrong and they were right. A Romantic Ireland had perhaps once existed, but it would only have been wild, free and romantic for some.

As for Donal Ryan's slightly altered stance, Barnabas Salmon suspected that he was simply becoming more open to the possibility that honesty and simplicity were not the same thing, and that many people who had been caught in the teeth of the Tiger, had been honest rather than stupid. Ryan still took issue with Salmon's assertion that there was a clear, discernible link between the abuse scandal and the economic meltdown. According to Salmon, the former owed its genesis to a group of misfits who had perverted sacred teaching in a bid to terrorise the population into submission under the threat of hellfire. The latter had economically wrecked the country, sending many to an early grave in the process, because of their warped interpretation of what a free market constitutes. What united them both were abuses of trust and power.

Ryan was contemptuous of what he considered was Salmon's over emotional opinion. The two issues, he insisted, were chalk and cheese by nature. Both scandals had been caused by a few bad apples and it was wrong, and what was more, unchristian to tarnish the reputation of the innocent.

He couldn't help suspecting that the thespian in Salmon was coming to the fore, and that for all his outward display of angst and pity, he was really rather enjoying the drama of it all. In Ryan's opinion, the media and some others were revelling in the emotional outpourings of people whose economic sails had been trimmed.

In this, Ryan had the wrong measure of Barnabas Salmon, for the rural gentleman could barely tolerate listening to the media and never bought a newspaper. No one needed the mass media to tell them how bad things had become. The carnage was visible everywhere in the form of abandoned houses, closed shops and small traders left unpaid. As far as Salmon was concerned, the media were merely milking the situation for stories of gloom and doom because they were easy pickings. As in the case of the simmering abuse scandal, it was the meek and socially insignificant people who were carrying the brunt of the downturn. What was needed now was a brave new voice to cry out from the wilderness.

So, the Saturday after the IMF entered Ireland, when the consequences of their mission was becoming a little more transparent, Salmon began his sermon feeling less than adequate to the challenge being presented.

'I know that many of you are not in an easy place right now,' he began, 'with the financial situation of the country placing so many of you in difficult positions. The thought of a man without a mortgage or a family to support preaching to you may not seem like an edifying prospect.

'How frightening and doom-laden the words of tonight's gospel sound. "The foolish man who built his house upon the sand, and the rain fell and the floods came and the wind blew and they beat upon the house and it fell and great was that fall."'

Those who had not been paying attention when the gospel had been read, now heard the words with a startling clarity, and found them less than encouraging.

'Take a look at the ceiling of this church,' Salmon said, raising his own head to look up, 'see how the beams are constructed; do you not find them reminiscent of an upturned boat? What an analogy for this moment in time. We are in the water and it is imperative that we get out.'

'The words in tonight's gospel are, of course, metaphorical, and this is most certainly not going to be a sermon about the wisdom or folly of having bought a house, or having extended a business. I want to talk to you about the mentality of the individual and something that I think has a degree of relevance to this situation. The concept I have in mind is what the poet Keats called "negative capability." In layman's terms, it simply means the ability to simultaneously acknowledge the unpredictable nature of events, while conducting oneself with confidence and happiness. In other words, to be capable of living with uncertainties

'For too many people in this country, the economic crash will signify personal failure, while for some it might herald the start of a new adventure.

'It is an unpalatable fact that bad news sells, hence the glut of it in the papers, but when all is said and done, the media is merely a business, and as in all business, fact and fiction are often interchangeable. No matter how dark the days ahead may appear at this moment, some good will come from it. For some, this recession will mark the start of a new life on a distant shore that will prove enhancing and life affirming. Emigration does not have to cause guilt, for either those who go, or those who stay. That is one of the very real benefits of the twenty first century; it has the possibility to be very different from the emigration of days gone by. This recession will also free some people from relationships that have the potential for bad, and while it will test marriages, it cannot break them. Only the people involved can do that.

'The past year has been one long story of an establishment that abused its mission, and there is every danger that this economic devastation could strengthen another establishment to rule beyond its remit. Nothing empowers a government more than a compliant, defeated population; and what better tools are there for mandating compliance, than making people feel they are weak and powerless?

'No matter where this recession goes, it will not rival the horrors of the famine, the war of independence, or the civil war. Your ancestors faced greater trials, and by saying that I do not trivialise the heartbreak of today.

'No one who really knows Christ can be driven to despair and thoughts of death as a result of money. Those who claim they are might know *of* him, but crucially they don't *know* him. Hence, the demons he cast out from people, cried his name, and as did the people who taunted him when he was on the cross, with cries of "he saved others but cannot save himself." They all knew of him, but they did not know him. They had no relationship with him.

'Some years ago, when I served at a parish in a very leafy suburb of London, some parishioners informed me of a well-known celebrity who lived in the area. Now this man was a much loved television personality, and I'd say more than a few of you will know of him, and probably admire him tremendously for his joviality. However, the daughter of a parishioner of mine worked in his household and she confided that the man, in reality, was something of a brute. I have no reason to doubt her. As I stayed in the locality, many people, such as tradesmen, confirmed that the man was nothing like his screen persona. You see, most people in England knew of this man, but few really knew him.

'Yes, money talks, but do not elevate it. Without doubt, it can facilitate happiness, but it can also inflict huge misery when it says "goodbye."

'Victor Hugo stated: "adversity makes men, prosperity makes monsters". There is more than a grain of truth in that. Ireland, as a country, collectively put its trust in politicians, the clergy, bankers and developers, and it has been gravely let down. Cut out the middleman, place your trust and your hope only in God.

'Remember how I once told you that there are times when we enter the forest? Well this is one of them, and you have to believe that you will emerge strengthened not weakened. And, when the time comes and politicians seek your vote, remember this story. A small child tucked up in bed said to her grandmother. "Granny do all fairy tales begin with once upon a time?"

"No darling," replied the old woman, "there are a whole series of fairy tales that begin with 'If I am elected, I promise…'"

The impact of his sermon was far greater than Barnabas Salmon could have foretold, and it resulted in more parishioners than ever seeking him out as someone to whom they could confide their hopes and fears. Some called at the presbytery while others just happened to catch him on the beach. To each he offered a listening ear and a considered opinion, if one was sought, and to all, boundless encouragement. Many still found it difficult to articulate how it was that an English priest, with a cut glass accent that epitomised his comfortable background, managed to draw the wounded to him. By comparison, Father Ryan appeared distinctly detached as he continued to demonstrate his view that he existed to listen to their sins, and not to their business - oblivious to the fact that the two were often irreversibly connected.

As the year slowly turned there was no shortage of tragic stories concerning people submerged under a burden of too much misery. Many well-established family businesses were forced into bankruptcy while a whole range of enterprises, which had started so brightly at the dawn of the new era, floundered, leaving a trail of destruction.

However, there were also some happier outcomes. The outlook for old Sam Dunne, who lived with his money-minded daughter and son-in-law, had looked very grim for a while. The much talked about planning permission for a small estate of holiday homes had been sought and approved just prior to the economic meltdown and the next battle had been to persuade Sam that he would be better off in an old folk's home on the outskirts of the town. Alerted by Sam, Salmon had visited more frequently, and while he noted that the old man looked frailer, he had lost none of his fighting spirit. Salmon had also noted that Sam's daughter, Anne, looked more harassed than ever. She had set her stall out, and since she associated retreat with weakness was afraid to back down. Salmon never asked her to rethink her decision regarding her father, but he did engineer several conversations that caused her to look back with nostalgia to the happy days of her childhood when her father had farmed the land. It came as no great surprise when Salmon received a phone call one day from an exuberant Sam, who told him that God most surely did work in mysterious ways. In view of the recession, and for *undisclosed* personal reasons, Anne and Noel had wisely decided against the holiday homes. Instead, they were going to diversify into more specialised breeds of cattle. Noel's sister had a contact in England who was looking for a supplier of artisan lines to both restaurants and supermarkets, and who knew more about the rearing of cattle than Sam Ryan?

Not long after this joyful news, Eddie Moran, the schoolteacher called to the presbytery to see Father Barnabas.

'I wanted you to be the first to know Father,' he had told the surprised looking priest. 'Carolyn and I are leaving the area. We both have work permits for Australia, and after that we intend to travel and see a bit of the world.'

'Well my goodness me,' Salmon had exclaimed. 'What a surprise. Might I ask what brought this about?'

Eddie had laughed, 'I think you might know, or at least be up to making a good guess about that. I have thought many things through since having that talk with you. I have acted as a very immature man, and I have tried to make an effort to think constructively.'

'Oh Eddie,' Salmon had counselled, 'please don't talk like that. You are a fine young fellow. I sincerely hope this decision is not a result of any pressure I might have put on you. What does Carolyn make of it all?'

'Well Father,' Eddie replied conspiratorially, 'you did put pressure on me, pressure that I didn't want but pressure I needed to man-up. Carolyn's parents, especially her father, have never liked or trusted me, but if you think about some of the things I told you, they were probably right to be wary and if I hadn't met you, I may well have proved them to be spot on.'

'Everyone has doubts and fears Eddie,' Salmon replied, 'they are supremely human things to experience, and you went the extra mile by seeking help. Tell me, what does Carolyn think of it all?'

'I was honest with her, probably for the first time. I remembered you asking me how I would have felt if she had dumped me prior to the wedding, and the truth is I would have been devastated. I think, Father, it was all about control. Once the wedding was over, I felt I had no say; I was trapped and I expected Carolyn to read my mind, because I thought I was reading hers; only I wasn't, at least not correctly.'

'And what made you see that you weren't?'

'A lot of things, after reflecting on the things you said, I came to see that we had both handed control to others. We were not building a life together; we were shifting into one that was being built for us. Carolyn believes that going away it will be like a courtship again, just the two of us, dependent on each other, and I agree.'

'Then bon voyage Eddie,' the priest had said. 'May you have a long and happy journey together.'

'You'll be the first person we call on when we come back,' Eddie had said, as he had taken his leave.

Salmon had smiled but said nothing.

Later that same evening he chanced upon a discussion Father Ryan and Madge Healy were having, and he caught the tail end of what Madge was saying, 'Can you believe that? In the middle of a recession as well.'

'Now, that sounds interesting,' he had commented.

'Shocking more like Father Salmon,' Madge had replied primly. 'Eddie Moran is giving up his job at the school, and Carolyn has given notice to the bank.'

He bit back a desire to say, 'tell me news not history,' and merely smiled.

'It is no joke Father,' she said annoyed at his failure to look shocked, 'you can understand some people emigrating, I mean if they have no job, but for a pair like them who have everything, to throw that up to see the world, well it is madness.'

'What good is it to win the world and lose your soul,' Salmon replied, 'they are a fine young couple and Droumbally will always be here for them, but their youth and their dreams will not. Good luck to the pair of them, I say.'

Madge Healy fixed a look of scorn on him. She had a suspicion that the English priest had had a hand in the whole affair. Father Ryan said nothing, but he did think someone ought to tell Barnabas to go easy on the fairy tales.

Later that same evening, as Madge prepared herself to settle in for the night, she caught a glimpse of the handsome features of her deceased husband staring out from the photo, which she kept on display for propriety's sake. As she stared into his face, she saw the image of her sons emerge from his features. Her thoughts turned to them, considering what they might be doing in New York. They had left on the cusp of the Celtic Tiger and had ignored all her pleadings to stay. Weeks after their arrival in America, they had sent her a joint letter telling her that the memories they retained of their father were the reason for their departure.

Without warning, Madge Healy experienced a rare moment of enlightenment. She recognised in that instant that the bitterness that nestled in her heart was responsible for the spite she now felt towards Eddie and Carolyn Moran. Just like her children, they were spurning the chance of a comfortable and familiar life for the possibility of a meaningful one. She had settled for complacency; she had enjoyed a career and had married a local man who had owned land, but while she had loved, she had never felt loved in return. All told, she had made a poor bargain; she had, as her late mother had put it, bought the coal and failed to warm herself. For the first time since her sons' departure for America, Madge Healy cried. Her tears fell for lost opportunity. She had settled for security and peace of mind, but neither were ever a realistic prospect with a husband who was incapable of loving. She could and she should have made a stand, taken a chance. If she had, there was every possibility that her sons would be in Ireland now.

With great reluctance, Madge had to admit that the English priest was right. Dreams and youth did not last forever and the tragedy was that some people, like her, only realised it when it was too late. She had an overwhelming desire to run to Barnabas Salmon and ask him what should she do; how could she possibly turn the tide? As the panic of despair hit her, she thought back to something else the rural gentleman had once said, way back when he had delivered his first sermon: "it is never too late to have a happy childhood." Could he be right? As she hesitated, the words he had uttered upon hearing the news about Eddie and Carolyn's departure replayed themselves in her mind: 'Droumbally will always be here for them.' It would always be here for her as well. Why not blow caution to the wind and book a ticket for America? She would naturally call in and see James and Oliver, and then have an adventure of her own down the West Coast. What and who was to stop her?

Ever since his meeting with Eddie Moran, Salmon had seen that the choice for the newly wedded couple had been a stark one. Either the two ambled along until they drifted apart at diverging paths in the woods, or they made a joint decision to throw their hats into the ring and become masters of their own fate. Salmon's heart delighted in the decision they had made.

Many of the young people leaving for the UK, Canada and Australia in the 21st century were canaries escaping the pit and could not be compared to those who had fled in previous centuries. Their going was still traumatic for their parents, but this had been mitigated by cheaper flights and innovations in telecommunications. The real tragedy resided with the people who were buried in debt with no possibility of escape. The media focused sentimentally on the emotional comings and goings at Dublin airport, but far less sympathy was shown for the trapped; because debt, unlike adventure, is never enviable.

Chapter Twenty

End Times

The trials and tribulations that had filled the last few years of the first decade of the new millennium took their toll on a great many people, not least Father Barnabas Salmon. As the winter of 2010 progressed, he had a recurrence of the many ailments that had besieged him since his childhood. The parishioners remarked amongst themselves on how painfully thin he looked and how much slower he now walked. Even his previously arrow-straight posture was starting to stoop.

He told the parish one Saturday night that he had every expectation that Clarissa would visit Ireland and would stay in the parish sometime early in 2011.

Although his physical form was beginning to let him down, his mind and voice remained as sharp as the day he had arrived. He was now generally considered something of a local treasure.

He no longer had cause to visit England, and the congregation missed the stories with which he had once regaled them upon his return. He settled instead for reading extracts, as appropriate, from the letters Clarissa sent him, which contained wry observations on a Kentish way of life.

He told them once that whenever he read the advice Jesus gave concerning the wisdom of choosing the lowest position at a feast or wedding so that the host might say, 'come friend move up to a better place,' he felt certain that the good Lord must have West Cork ancestry. It was while on the subject of achieving the heart's desire by employing subtle and understated means that he relayed to them a story Clarissa had told him in her latest letter. It concerned a young man who belonged to a fundamentalist sect.

'Now, before relaying this story,' he explained, 'I want to tell you that I make no judgement, because such people genuinely seek God, and those who are not against us are surely for us, but having said that, I remain extremely grateful for my own heritage.'

He paused before continuing, 'Anyway, this sect amongst its other decrees, absolutely forbids the watching of television, women are forbidden from wearing trousers or cutting their hair, bright colours are taboo and so on; so I think you get my drift. Well, Clarissa tells me that the English football team were playing a very important match, and she had called out a plumber, who turned out to be a fine young man. Now, she was unaware of his leanings, so thinking that like many others he would want to watch the game, she put the television on in the lounge and told him he was welcome to keep an eye on it. He nodded politely and began to get on with his job. Meanwhile, Clarissa took herself away to the conservatory on the other side of the house, but she could still hear the roar of the crowd. When she investigated, she saw that the young man had opened the glass doors that led from the kitchen. So, she tiptoed over very quietly to close them, and to her surprise, the young man said. "Ma'am, if you don't mind, I'd like to keep the doors ajar because you see, my religion forbids me from watching television, but I figure that if I can catch its reflection in the window, I am not really watching it, and so I can enjoy the match with a clear conscience."

Now, I think that illustrates why it is best to go easy with rules and regulations. They have their place, but when applied too harshly they encourage deviance, as we know too well, to our cost.'

In keeping with Salmon's assertion that life is lived forward and remembered backwards, the parishioners remembered the Christmas of 2010 as the time Barnabas Salmon knew his days in West Cork were coming to an end.

In spite of his physically weakened health, he maintained his calls to the sick, the lonely and the elderly. In comparison to the busy, frenzied atmosphere of the early days of the new century, an aura of subdued melancholy now hung over the entire area, as many people strove to keep a roof over their heads and food on the table. There were people who had nothing to spend, and others who did have money, but were wary of doing so for fear of stirring jealousy, dislike or suspicion. The rural gentleman remained accessible to all, but he naturally gravitated towards those in need of assurance.

Bridie Clancy, once the terror of the parish, had changed irrevocably since the priest had started visiting her regularly. The change came about slowly, but she was now finally up to casually acknowledging people she had once actively despised.

She too was a great deal frailer and just before Christmas she had to accept more assistance from a new home help. The doctor had advised Bridie that she would be better off in hospital, but she had reared up at the suggestion. So, Julia Cusack, a local mother and carer, along with a Polish girl, Anna Lemac, now took it in turns to call upon the old woman. Naturally, Barnabas Salmon was a more regular visitor than ever, but he still had to tie Wolf up outside the door, for Bridie could not abide dogs, no matter their size, shape or breed.

He would read stories to her, and the home helps, when both present, would grin at each other as they heard his dramatic booming voice reading the short stories of Frank O'Connor, Sean O'Faolain and the fairy tales of Hans Christian Andersen.

'Well, isn't he just the perfect performer Bridie?' Julia Cusack proclaimed one day, as she walked into the room to see Bride Clancy entranced by the tale of the steadfast Tin Soldier.

'As I said before, I'm not a perfectionist,' Barnabas Salmon told her with a smile, 'though my parents undoubtedly were.'

'See,' Julia said to Bridie as she adjusted the old woman's pillow, 'what luck we had in drawing an entertainer into the parish, a born storyteller no less.'

'I fear you will make me blush Julia,' Salmon told the home help, as he lifted himself gingerly from his chair. 'Bridie is testimony to my talent, just look at her.'

The priest and Julia looked at the old woman who was now sound asleep. 'She loves your visits Father,' the home help told him. 'Somehow you have injected joy into her life, and believe me, that is no mean achievement.'

Salmon reached over and lifted his cap from the table where he had left it, and walked softly to the door.

'She's determined to make it to midnight Mass,' Julia informed him as she saw him off at the door.

'I think she is eager to get into the good books of the Man upstairs.'

The midnight Mass of Christmas 2010, which Father Salmon celebrated thanks to Father Ryan agreeing to take the day Mass instead, was a very different affair to the first Christmas Mass of Salmon's ministry in West Cork. Back in 2007 he had regaled an affluent parish with tales of his childhood Christmas memories and had cheerily derided the comment made by a clergyman who had described Christmas as the Disneyfication of Christianity.

He now faced a congregation of people who felt neglected, overwhelmed, fearful and abandoned. One by one, they had witnessed all the things in which they had placed their trust crumble in the face of reality. But, they were a resilient people, and though many longed to lay their burdens down, commitment to family and a haunting residue of faith prevented them from doing so.

'Christianity,' he told them that cold winter night, 'should help us to face the music even when we don't like the tune that is being played. For people of no faith, Christmas must seem like the happiest time of year, and Easter the saddest time of all.

'But in truth, I do not think that people of faith can fail to see Christmas without the shadow of the cross. The child who enters the world through a humble birth, as we all know, grew up to be rejected by those he came to save, and the Madonna is humbled to see her son die a criminal's death.

'I cannot let this Christmas celebration go by without saying something about the role of Mary, the mother and the woman. She was not a docile participant, and I think the church has done her and if I might say, women in general a disservice by often portraying her as such.

'I would ask you to consider for one moment, the words of the Magnificat: "He has cast down the mighty from their thrones, / and has lifted up the lowly. / He has filled the hungry with good things, / and the rich he has sent away empty."

'This is powerful language. They are the words of a strong, committed woman, not the murmurings of a shrinking violet. Above all, it is a song of hope speaking of the triumph of God.

'Do not be misled by the still common caricature of women as insatiable for the things money can buy. It has no foundation in theology.

'At this moment in time, the boat is rocky for all of us. The waters are deep, and uneasy. We are assailed by secularists on all sides whose best offer is, "well I like the ethics but I don't do the mumbo jumbo."

'That, of course, is their perception, but just how wrong a perception it is. I recall an incident one day as a young teenager, when I caught sight of myself in a mirror dressed in the ridiculous uniform of the local public school, complete with blazer, and unturned collars, all topped off with a straw boater. I gazed into the mirror, and I thought I saw the very epitome of privilege.

'How poor my perception was, and how shallow my understanding proved to be. Parents, be warned when you buy or seek things for your child. Ask yourself: is it really for them, or does its charm rest in how good it makes you feel about yourself?

'Think carefully about your perception of Christmas. Do you fully see its link with the Easter story, or is it a party, a remnant from pagan days? Is it merely a festival to mark a happy time when the year is at its darkest?

'It will end on the 6th January with the arrival of the magi, and the New Year will unfold with all its highs and lows. Wherever you are spiritually right now, think on these words of Hans Christian Andersen. "My life is a lovely story and full of adventure", and make them prophetic.'

On the morning of the feast of the epiphany, also known as Women's Little Christmas, a feast that is frequently celebrated by women in Cork and Kerry, Father Barnabas received an urgent phone call. Bridie Clancy was dying. He hurried to the ramshackle old house up beyond Slattery's bar, taking with him all the things needed to anoint the old woman.

As the old woman drifted in and out of consciousness, he held her hand and spoke gently and reassuringly to her. Julia Cusack, along with another local woman was present. Anna Lemac had returned to Poland for a Christmas holiday. Between them, the two women carried to the parish the story of the remarkably peaceful demise of the old woman who had inspired so much fear and loathing over the course of her life.

'She was transformed,' Julia told Madge Healy, 'for the first time, I saw her smile and she looked almost saintly.'

'Whatever did he say to her?' Madge asked, 'and did she make a confession? You know he has very modern views like that, thinks it's all up to God.'

'I don't know,' Julia replied. 'I only caught a bare remnant of the actual conversation. She wasn't lucid at all times you see, sort of drifting in and out, but I did hear him say something about what did it matter if you are born in a duck yard if only you are hatched from a swan.'

'Really,' Madge replied, a little disdainfully, half hoping to have caught whiff of the scandal that had shadowed the old woman most of her life, 'and this from the fellow who was giving out about others and mumbo jumbo.' For all that Madge had conceded to herself that Salmon had some merits, she still couldn't refrain from criticism when she felt he was acting less than orthodox.

'It was strange, surreal even,' Julia conceded a little stiffly, 'but as far from mumbo jumbo as it gets. There was something really quite exquisite about it.' She paused for a moment as if to catch her emotion, for she had been touched by the gentleness of the priest, and Madge Healy's pernickety questioning irritated her. 'No wonder she never made it to principal', she thought crossly, 'minding mice at the crossroads would probably test her capabilities.'

'There was something else,' Mary Kelly, who was also present, insisted, 'Anita said she distinctly heard Bridie say to Father Barnabas, "I do not want to hear it, because to know too much might destroy my happiness."'

'Hear what?' Madge Healy asked querulously, but the other women ignored her.

In death, as in life, Bridie Clancy remained an enigma. Neither of the two women had heard Bridie Clancy's last words. Father Salmon had, and they had struck him to the core of his soul, for as she passed away, she had repeated the dying words of Tolstoy's beloved heroine, 'Lord, forgive me all.'

The church was not filled to capacity for the funeral of Bridie Clancy, but more people attended than once would have been dreamt possible.

Like others in the parish, she too had been influenced by the rural gentleman, and in the latter days of her life, something of her hidden heart had emerged.

The people whose job it had been to look after her as she had steadily grown too frail to look after herself testified that, just as the selfish giant had been transformed by the appearance of the Christ child into his life, so the selfish midget had blossomed under the care of the rural gentleman.

Father Salmon officiated at the burial, and although he pointed no fingers nor performed any whitewashing on the memory of the dead woman, not a single person was left unmoved by his words.

'No one knows the mind of God,' he told the mourners, 'and none of us know the heart or mind of each other. In fact, the rush to judgement leaves open the possibility of profound regrets.

'In this world we can witness perfection; the beauty of a star filled night and the setting sun on the water. We can also witness things that are far from perfection, such as illness, meanness of spirit and people who live without love. It is the imperfect however, that shows more clearly the existence of God. Every person we meet who appears to be a perfect example of imperfection provides us with an opportunity to develop love, understanding and gentleness.

'Remember the words of Chesterton, which I have mentioned before, but will mention again because of their value. "The bible tells us to love our neighbours and our enemies, probably because they are the same people."

'Is that not true of all of us, how many times do we alternate between being a neighbour and being an enemy?

'Do not judge Bridie. Do not judge anyone. For no matter how well you think you know the story of another, be assured, you only know the blurb.

'I often heard tales about Bridie. I heard she had a remarkable aim, not with a golf club unfortunately, but with crab apples, spuds and whatever came to hand.

'I also heard that she was forthright when telling canvassing politicians where to go, but I never heard a single person accuse her of having a gossiping tongue. Sometimes we can talk about the negative things people do, but conveniently fail to acknowledge the vices of which they are not guilty. Bridie, like all of us, had faults and failings, but no one could ever have accused her of being sanctimonious.

'She was never one to take people down to build up herself. I remember a conversation during which she told me how much she feared overly religious people. I knew exactly what she meant, and I suspect that most of you do as well. She put me in mind of St Teresa of Avila who said, "I do not fear the devil half as much as I fear those who fear him."

'All of which brings me to the central point of our existence, which is to aim to love as we are loved. The great Pope John Paul the first, who only reigned for thirty three days, said something that gave me great reassurance, and I can vouch that it gave great succour to Bridie as well, "God is our Father; even more He is our mother."

As we commit Bridie to the mercy of Christ, let us pray the prayer of the good thief, "Lord, remember me when you come into your kingdom." Remember all of us, O Lord, and judge us not according to our desert, but according to thy mercy.'

The funeral Mass made a great impression on how the people of the village remembered Bridie Clancy. Those who had been subjected to her bitter tongue, while still able to recall and recoil at her unpleasantness, tempered their memory in the light of Father Barnabas Salmon's sermon. In fact, the more they reflected on his words, the more they came to believe that there must have been more to the old woman than had met the eye.

One thing was for certain, Barnabas Salmon was party to her history and the reason for her change of heart, and their admiration for him grew as it dawned on them that he was a nurturing influence. Like dieters who sometimes ask the question, "do I really need to eat this?" before indulging in a deliciously wicked treat, many in the vicinity now found themselves questioning the need to hear or repeat certain things with the injunction, what would Salmon make of this?

Bridie Clancy was laid to rest in the churchyard of the village church, and since she had no living relatives, or at least none that could be acknowledged, she was buried without a headstone, as insignificant in death as she had been in life.

Chapter Twenty-One

The Knowledge of Salmon

Barnabas Salmon's expectation that Clarissa would visit Ireland sometime in the early part of 2011 proved prophetic. On the morning of Friday the 25th March, as some parishioners gathered in the church of the Faithful Virgin in anticipation of celebrating Mass, the rural gentleman was found dead by Father Donal Ryan. He was sitting in his favourite armchair in the very living room where he had made welcome so many visitors who had come to seek his counsel. The books of his beloved Hugo and Tolstoy lay scattered at his feet, and in his right hand, he held the bookmark of St Teresa of Avila.

Let nothing disturb you,
Let nothing frighten you,
All things are passing;
God only is changeless.
Patience gains all things.
Who has God wants nothing.
God alone suffices.

Nestled carefully under his chair, no doubt keeping a dutiful watch over his master, sat the ever-faithful Wolf.

As a child, Barnabas Salmon had suffered from acute pleurisy, the effects of which had plagued him with ill health for most of his life, and his heart had quite suddenly given up on him. In retrospect, those who knew him best realised that intuitively, he had known since Christmas that his mission on this earth was near its end. This was evident from the letters he had written and various comments he had made. There was some solace to be had, however, in the knowledge that providence had seen fit for his demise to take place on the feast day of St Dismas, the so-called Good Thief. Father Salmon had always claimed him as his special and powerful patron saint and inspiration.

Shock and soul shaking despondency greeted the news of his death. It was almost impossible to believe that the loud booming voice of the rural gentleman would never again hail a greeting, and that the sight of him walking the hills and boreens with the faithful little dog at his side would never again be witnessed. Who would tend to the lonely, the sick and the elderly now?

With Father Barnabas Salmon no longer present, members of the parish realised with lucidity his role as an honest broker, the human bridge he had presented between people and church; the word made accessible. The ear and mind of a trusted confidant were forever closed, and a great sense of loss descended on a people who felt very much like "sheep without a shepherd when the snow blocks out the sky."

Father Donal Ryan was shaken and bewildered at the outpouring of shock and grief caused by the sudden passing of Barnabas Salmon, and to his credit, he acknowledged immediately that he had severely underestimated the stature of the man. From the very moment he had set his eyes on him, he had known that they were destined to be colleagues but never close friends. Upon his death, however, he looked back, not on the shortcomings of a man he had never really understood, but on his own shortcomings. He had always seen himself as a man of the people, he was of their stock and shared their interests and passions, but he had never won their hearts in the way the outsider had.

If Barnabas Salmon were alive, he would have informed Ryan that the reason why he had never won the hearts of his people was because he had never sought to do so. With Salmon dead and with the gift of hindsight, Ryan regretted that he had paid so little attention to the method the priest had employed to make his vocation so relevant to the lives of the people he had served.

People from the entire area and beyond, flocked to the requiem Mass for the dearly loved priest. Catholic, Protestant and those of no denomination at all came to acknowledge the passing of a great man. Even Ger O'Reilly turned up with his distraught niece. The presbytery had been inundated with telephone calls and enquiries from various parishes in England where Father Salmon had served in the past. However, as the death had occurred on a Friday, few from abroad were able to attend the Sunday funeral. One of the few exceptions of course was Clarissa Allan-Lowry.

Word had quickly spread through the assembled congregation that the vivacious, petite woman with the silver blonde hair, dressed in a dark, perfectly tailored skirt and jacket, was none other than Clarissa. Heads turned to acknowledge the woman they all felt they had come to know so well.

She was accompanied by a tall serious looking young man who was also dressed sombrely, but who did not look as comfortable with his surroundings as the woman did. Both possessed a natural air of dignity, and the woman seemed genuinely touched by the people who had recognised her.

Naturally, Father Brendan O'Sullivan, as a long-standing friend of Father Barnabas, was the main concelebrant at the requiem Mass.

He began his sermon by telling the assembled people some background information about their beloved priest, and most of it was fairly innocuous.

'When I first met Barnabas, you won't be surprised to hear that he told me a story. He told me about a visit he had made to a parish primary school somewhere in south London. He said that he had asked the children a few questions about the Mass; why they went and who served and so on. He then asked them why it was important to be quiet in church, and a small child put up her hand and said, "Because people are sleeping."

'As you can imagine, that tickled Barnabas enormously, but it also made him think. All of you know perfectly well, that when Barnabas spoke, even the dead stood little chance of sleep, and not just on account of that chiselled booming voice, but because, for Barnabas, every word mattered.

'He took the salvation of his flock seriously, and he was inspired by many great writers. It wasn't just the actor in him that sparked his interest in literature, or indeed the literature itself. His attraction to, or should I say fascination with the likes of Victor Hugo, Leo Tolstoy, Sigrid Undset and of course Hans Christian Andersen, was mainly driven by the life stories of these great writers, which in the main, were complex, disorderly and some might say downright scandalous. What Barnabas perceived in them was their desire, as individuals, to impart to the world stories concerning the heroics of the human soul; the triumph of God-fearing people who struggled to be virtuous.. He recognised and sincerely believed that for many people, no matter their doctrine, salvation was theirs, because what mattered to God was their longing; their personal search for perfection in an imperfect world.

'Barnabas was very clear about the reading he wanted you to hear today. The words of St Matthew's gospel, chapter six and verses twenty four to thirty four epitomised the belief and the hope by which he lived his life. It goes without saying that the tenor of this gospel passage appealed to his theatrical nature with its evocative language regarding the birds of the sky, and the flowers in the field. The essence of his devotion to this reading was its exhortation that no one can be the slave of two masters, and the futility of worrying about tomorrow.

'Barnabas was a man who was dealt many cruel blows and troubles during the course of his life, but he survived, for he was the willing slave of the one true master. All of us who were blessed to have known him were the benefactors of that love.'

The Mass continued to its conclusion, but just before the body was to be taken from the church to its final resting place in the surrounding churchyard, Clarissa Lowry-Allan was invited by the parish priest, Father Donal Ryan, to address the congregation.

'Thank you,' she said, turning her head to acknowledge the priest, 'for your kind permission in allowing me to address the congregation. I understand that it was your prerogative to refuse my request, and I am grateful for your kind agreement.' Her voice was clear and confident, and though not booming, it still reached to the back of the church.

'Everything I want to say to you all today has the blessing and consent of Barnabas and the permission of your parish priest. As Father O'Sullivan alluded in his sermon, there is much of which you may not be aware concerning the life of Barnabas Salmon, and it was his dying wish that I should tell you some things he wanted you to know; things he could not share with you during his lifetime.

'It gave him great pleasure to be known amongst you as the rural gentleman, though I gathered from what he said that the title was intended as an affectionate nickname, and had not been intended for his ears.' A gentle murmur of approval ran through the church.

'Barnabas loved the rural life. He felt closer to God and closer to his calling when surrounded by a flowing stream, a star filled sky or a simple flower in full bloom. He took them all as signs of God's presence in a lovely though lonely world.'

She paused, and not a single member of the congregation seated in front of the altar was aware of the bombshell she was about to launch.

'I first met Barnabas when I was about seven years old.' A ripple of unease bordering on fear began to make its way around the church, as everyone wondered about what next was going to be revealed. Clarissa immediately became aware of the rise in tension and paused again before continuing.

'Please do not let your hearts be troubled. As I speak, keep in mind all the things that Barnabas ever told you. Recall in your own hearts how he introduced me to you by referring to me as his sister in Christ. You see, Barnabas Salmon was the adopted son of parents who lived in dire poverty in the east end of London.

'We met as children when he came with his family every year to pick the hops on a nearby farm. From the moment I met him, I knew I was in the company of a very special person, and our relationship from that time has been that of a loving brother and sister.

'Think back to all the things Barnabas ever told you about his childhood; did you ever wonder that he never specifically talked about his mother or father? The childhood that Barnabas remembered so affectionately and even shared occasionally, was mine.

All of you, I am sure, know how much he loved Hans Christian Andersen. As a child, I was given a copy of Andersen's fairy tales and sometimes Barnabas and I would read those wonderful stories together and it was like being taken away to a magical world. You will know that one of his favourite sayings from Andersen was, "Everyone's life is a fairy tale written by God." Well those words were to prove more accurate than we could ever have guessed as children. The greatest irony, is that of all the stories Hans Christian Andersen ever told, the one that had the greatest impact on Barnabas when he was a child, was a story called, "She was Good for Nothing," which is the tale of a poor, suffering mother who had an illegitimate son. He had a great fear that it might prove prophetic.

'Some years ago, I was commissioned by a London based newspaper to research the subject of illegitimacy in the Ireland of the 1940's, and the role of the Church in the care of these children. It might come as an enormous shock to you to learn that in the process of my research, I came across the mother of Barnabas Salmon. I had known for a long time that he was anxious to discover who his mother really was, and when I made the discovery, I could not in truth keep it from him. It was his right to know.

'You see the real mother of Barnabas gave birth to him at the age of fifteen in very unhappy circumstances. She was a child and a victim, and subjected to much cruelty, particularly by people who should have known so much better by virtue of their age and calling. She had tried to escape with her child, determined to make a life with him, but had been apprehended on the road that leads west from the city.

'I know that the issue of clerical abuse and the role of the church in some very unhappy history in Ireland troubled Barnabas deeply, but he was never blind to the untold truth about the many great things that were also done by that same church. It was with the aid of the church hierarchy that Barnabas was able to see out his days in this beautiful area, after a lifetime of ill health, and it is by the kind permission of your parish priest that I am able to deliver this obituary to Barnabas today.

'The name Barnabas, which he chose upon entering the priesthood, can translate to mean, "Sons of consolation" or "sons of encouragement." He came back here to meet his mother, and to console her in her last years through a happy, exaggerated depiction of his childhood. While he had grown up with fearful thoughts of his mother being unhappy, she too, as I discovered, had lived in fear and misery, convinced that her child had been given over to a cruel and unhappy existence. His aim, from the moment he came to Droumbally, was to reassure his mother's bruised heart and soul that, far from being the victim of a cruel and unhappy adoption, he had in fact lived in the heart of luxury.

'The truthful reality unfortunately, was that Barnabas suffered terrible abuse from his adoptive parents. He was taunted about his heritage, beaten and neglected, and subjected to levels of extreme cruelty. There was a good reason why Barnabas always declined milk in his tea or coffee, it was the habit of his adoptive father to spit in the milk bottle every morning, knowing that the child would then choose to go without. Barnabas never displayed self-pity, not even as a child. His pity was invariably for those who had been given more, but who failed to utilize it. I remember one occasion when, at my instigation, Barnabas tried on the school uniform of my brother Piers who attended a highly esteemed public school. Turning to me, with the tie askew and the boater on back to front, he said, "don't I look the very epitome of privilege?"

He told me some years later how he regretted ever uttering those words, for you see, Piers, in spite of having it all, lived a brief and unhappy life.' She paused again in deference to her brother before resuming in a more uplifting tone of voice.

'At the age of seventeen, I was sent to a finishing school in Switzerland, and Barnabas and I did not meet again for another three years. During that time, he had enrolled at a stage school whilst working by day as a porter in a hospital in central London. He was handsome, articulate and every bit as charming as the day I first met him. I fell deeply in love with my childhood friend, but I am afraid my parents made life very difficult for us. They had been happy to welcome Barnabas as a child and teenager in need of charity, but as a son in law, that was quite unthinkable.

'It was not their opposition that forestalled our romance, however. One evening, while returning home from a play where he had been cast as an understudy, Barnabas called into a church near the Strand, and had what can only be called a "road to Damascus experience." He chanced upon a meditation on the words spoken between Christ and the good thief, and as he told me afterwards, they confirmed in his own heart the necessity of believing that it is never too late. He was called, and being Barnabas, the moment he set his hand to the plough, our romance was over.

'It took a long time and a lot of research to find his mother, and the story of her life almost broke his heart.

Andersen's story of 'She was Good for Nothing' had been made real.

'He could not contemplate compounding her misery by letting her know that her intuition concerning his life story had been accurate. Yes, she had indeed been betrayed, not just by her family who forsook her in her hour of need, but also by people working under the auspices of the church, who betrayed her child by handing him into the care of people immune to love and kindness. As the years went by, she became increasingly bitter and obstinate, to the point that she even denied ever having had a child because that was easier than fearing what had become of him.

'But his mission on coming back to the place of his birth was not just to console his mother, but to reach out to her community, to tell them first-hand of the dangers invited by an insular, closed approach to life. His invocation was and always has been, "Then cherish pity lest you drive an angel from your door."

'As Father Brendan said in his sermon today, Barnabas believed, very clearly, that no one can ever be the servant of two masters. Working with the Irish community in London, he discovered that many were indeed the slaves of two masters, torn between old ways and the chance of a new life. He often pondered whether anyone would ever spot him as a cuckoo, or indeed a salmon returning to the place of his birth.

'You were loved very dearly by him. He wanted nothing more from you than the very tall order of requesting your help to build a community that could only see each other through the eyes of God.

'Barnabas had been ill many times, and the fact that he survived his mother is, in its own way, nothing short of a miracle. He knew that Bridie Clancy was so very afraid of meeting her God alone, but God, at the very last minute, did not let her down.

'He left me with one very last request: some time ago he preached a sermon on the scourge of suicide. He asked me to reassure you of his belief that a tragic end of a life should never be taken as a sign of eternal tragedy in the next. Barnabas, his mission completed, accepted by you, loved by you, was happy to at last go home, truly home.'

Epilogue

Barnabas Salmon continued to be remembered and spoken about long after his departure from West Cork. As he had prophesied, the parish had lived the journey with him, so they would remember him backwards.

With the knowledge of his own deprived background set against the backdrop of his mother's life story, they finally understood why he had alluded to "the man who never was" during his first Mass in the parish. Torn from his mother, his country and his heritage, how could he have ever truly known who he was?

"Who am I?" was therefore the question he asked throughout his life, and it is a question that he believed everyone should ask of themselves. For Barnabas Salmon, knowledge of self, in all its many facets, was the pathway to knowing something about the meaning of existence, and emotion far from being an impediment to reason was, in his opinion, just another feature of it.

He was a man who used his disadvantage to the advantage of others. A man who lived with the recognition that the greatest desire of every human being is the validation that they matter, that in some measure their existence is felt by another. This is why troubled people gravitated towards him, for in their innermost hearts they recognised a kindred spirit.

He arrived as a stranger, and left as a much-loved shepherd who taught, without resorting to the threat of justice, that nothing happens by chance and everything is a possibility for God.

Acting on the will and testament of the late Barnabas Salmon, a headstone was eventually placed on Bridie Clancy's grave which is situated in the far corner of the church yard under the partial shade of a rowan tree. It reads, "Here rests Bridget Clancy, the dearly beloved mother of Barnabas Salmon who fell asleep on the feast of the epiphany in the year of Our Lord, 2011."

Adjacent to her, in the space allotted for the priests of the church, rests the son who lived in the shadows of her life. Now they are united, testimony to the rural gentleman's belief that Victor Hugo had it right when he said:

"Our life dreams the utopia,
our death achieves the Ideal."

The End

Lightning Source UK Ltd.
Milton Keynes UK
UKOW02f2151021215

263985UK00001B/19/P